THORNE, Matt

Kingmaker's castle

by the same author

39 Castles: BOOK ONE
GREENGROVE CASTLE

Matt Thorne has published six adult novels to widespread critical acclaim, co-edited the anthology *All Hail the New Puritans*, and is a regular reviewer for the *Independent on Sunday*. This is his second children's book.

39 Castles: BOOK TWO

KINGMAKER'S CASTLE

Matt Thorne

faber and faber

First published in 2005
by Faber and Faber Limited
3 Queen Square London WC1N 3AU

Typeset by Faber and Faber
Printed in England by Mackays of Chatham plc,
Chatham, Kent

A CIP record for this book
is available from the British Library

ISBN 0–571–21998–5

For Philippa Milnes-Smith
and Suzy Jenvey

Kingmaker's Secrets

Knowledge is Power

1 We are living in a new
  Dark Age.

2 The world was not always
  like this.

3 The world will not always
  be like this.

4 One day, order will be
  restored.

Castle Six: The Members

Jonathan: the new leader. Eleanor's father. Long, sandy hair. Dresses in old work-clothes, and is a kind man, but still getting used to his new position.

Alexandra: the female leader. She is in her mid-twenties with fine, honey-coloured hair and blue eyes. She is trustworthy and considerate.

Sarah: the great-great-granddaughter of the last princess before the fall of the kingdom. She is serene, reserved and full of secrets.

Lucinda: she used to work in an Inn. Kind to Eleanor and always sympathetic, but a young-seeming adult.

Zoran: the joker of the group. Always looking for a good night out, and not to be trusted with even the simplest tasks.

Robert: Zoran's sidekick. He is more careful than his friend, but is still liable to cause chaos. He has blond curly hair and is in his mid-twenties.

CASTLE FACTFILES

Plan

Top Floor

Ground Floor

KinDer Castle

Facts and Figures

> **Community population:** 300, all children
> **Language spoken:** English
> **Number of schools:** none
> **Size of army:** the entire population
> **Access to castle:** open to all
> **Currency:** sweets
> **Castle library:** abandoned

Plan

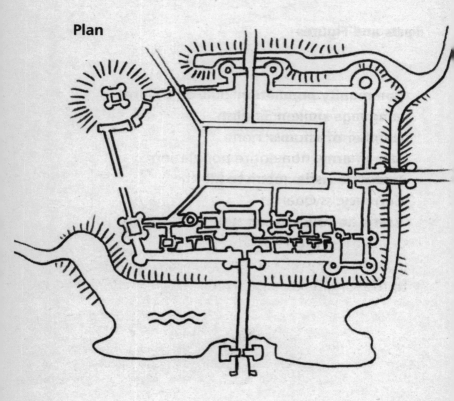

Kingmaker's Castle

Facts and Figures

Community population: 2000
Language spoken: English
Number of schools: 1
Size of army: none
Access to castle: restricted to the
Kingmaker's Quartet
Currency: none, barter system
Castle library: one of the largest
in the country, but access restricted
to the Kingmaker's Quartet

KINGMAKER'S CASTLE

This book takes place in a future that seems like the past. After the fall of the kingdom, everyone in England has divided themselves into thirty-nine communities, each arranged around a different castle, apart from those who have chosen to live in the wilderness . . .

PROLOGUE

Mary Reece often argued with her parents. They were a deeply suspicious couple, and usually assumed, without any evidence, that their daughter was up to no good. It wasn't that her parents were particularly cruel, but there were many misunderstandings on both sides and their relationship had hardened into one of mutual mistrust.

Today had been especially embarrassing. Recently, Mary had joined a group who hung out together after school by a river on the outskirts of their community. Her mother had begun to notice the muddy marks on her dresses and petticoats and questioned how her clothes had ended up in this condition. Mary had lied, telling her mother that she'd changed her route home, which was also a handy explanation for why she was arriving home an hour later than usual. Her mother had complained, but Mary protested that she needed the exercise and she let the matter drop. Now Mary spent every day longing for the end of school and the thirty minutes of peace she'd get lying with the others on the grass and listening to an older boy playing an acoustic guitar. While he played she would stare at the sky, her long red hair spread out behind her as she wondered what it would be like to live among the clouds.

This spot was supposed to be a secret. The children who came here didn't want the rest of the community to know about it, and you had to be invited to join the group. The area was guarded by a tall boy who wore a floppy hat and sat in the branches of an ash tree. Today he had raised the alarm by shouting 'Someone's coming!' Mary sat up, curious to see who had come here. It hadn't occurred to her that it might be her own mother. When she saw that was exactly who it was, Mary was horrified. Although her mother looked angry, Mary wasn't scared. She knew her mother would be cross about her hiding here, and disappointed by her lies, but Mary also felt she wasn't doing anything *that* wrong. She was more worried that the group would feel she'd betrayed them, and she'd be forbidden from joining them again.

The atmosphere in Mary's house was so tense that evening that she went to bed much earlier than usual, eager for a break from her mother's huffing and puffing. She got to sleep quickly, but at midnight she was awoken by some strange creaking sounds. It sounded as though someone was fiddling with the front door, but surely both her parents were asleep? She thought it might be a burglar and wondered what to do. Her parents would be cross if she woke them up and it was a false alarm, but what if someone really was breaking into their house?

Mary held her breath, straining to hear the noise. For a short moment, everything went quiet, and she assumed she had imagined the sounds. Then she heard someone running through the house and her bedroom door swung open. A tall man stood in front of her, a black mask over his face. He came over to Mary's bed and grabbed hold of her, bundling her under his arm. Then, all the while keeping a tight hold of her, he went through her cupboards and drawers, with one hand pulling out handfuls of her clothes and stuffing them into a brown sack. Mary froze in terror as the man turned his face towards her, pulling off his mask. She gasped in amazement. It was Anderson. He had changed so much since she last saw him. Although he'd always had long black hair and a thick beard, both had been well-groomed, without a trace of wildness. Now his hair was a tangled mess, his eyes were bloodshot, and his beard was long and scraggly.

He came towards Mary and took her in his arms. Mary trembled as he strode out of the house. Telling her to keep quiet, he placed her on the back of his horse. Then he mounted the animal himself, and jerked the reigns, riding off into the distance.

Chapter One

Eleanor awoke from a nightmare. She was in an unfamiliar room, at an inn far beyond the borders of her community. Travel was still a strange phenomenon for her, and she frequently had premonitions of danger. But tonight's nightmare had been about the people she had left behind. One of her friends was in trouble, but she couldn't see who it was. The face in the dream had been shrouded, and she heard several people sobbing at the same time. She suddenly realised she needed to use the toilet, and wondered if she was brave enough to make her way down the corridor to the bathroom. She lay there for a moment longer, then screwed up all her courage and got out of bed.

Making her way across the room in the darkness, she reached the door and opened it as quietly as possible, not wanting to wake anyone. As she did so, she noticed a figure standing at the far end of the corridor. The light in the corridor was dim, but there was a candle opposite the open doorway, illuminating Sarah, the most enigmatic of her Castle Six colleagues. Sarah was wearing a silver nightdress and her light brown hair was tied up at the back. She didn't seem to have noticed Eleanor, absorbed as she was in tearing up an envelope. Eleanor waited in the darkness until Sarah went back into her room. Then she walked down the corridor, used the toilet, and came back out. Standing by the door to Sarah's room, she felt an irresistible urge to know what she'd been tearing up. She knew it was wrong to snoop like this, but almost before she realised what she was doing, Eleanor took the fragments of the envelope and letter and returned to her room.

Standing by the desk near her window and using the moonlight to see by, Eleanor reassembled the letter as best she could. It was some sort of invitation, although its meaning was cryptic:

THE DAUGHTERS 225TH ANNIVERSARY
The Daughters' Castle
42nd Week, Day One
Nightfall
R.S.V.P.

Eleanor stared at the invitation, wondering what it meant. They weren't going to the Daughters' Castle, they were going to the Kingmaker's Castle. And who were the daughters? Even the thick cream card that the invitation was printed on surprised her. Paper was a highly prized commodity in her community and she had never seen something so clearly expensive and luxurious.

Sarah was always secretive, and Eleanor had no doubt that there were lots of things she kept from the rest of the group. She felt guilty about betraying her trust, but also intrigued, and wondered if there was any way of bringing this up with Sarah without revealing what she'd done.

Eleanor was about to drop the invitation into her bin when she had a sudden panic that someone might discover she'd taken it. The thought of being seen as dishonest filled Eleanor with alarm. Looking down, she noticed a loose floorboard and used her nails to tug it up, dropping the pieces of the invitation into the dusty space beneath. Then she turned out her light and went to sleep.

Chapter Two

Mary's mother stirred in her sleep, disturbed by noises in her house. Getting out of bed, she went through their small house to her daughter's bedroom. Startled by the empty bed and the clothes strewn across the floor, she hurried back to her bedroom and woke her husband.

'What is it?' he demanded.

'Mary's missing.'

He sat up and stared at her. 'What?'

'We need help. The Castle Six.'

'What are you talking about?' he asked, shaking his head. 'They're not there to help people like us.'

'Jonathan loves Mary; he'll know what to do.'

Mary's father gazed into the darkness. Her mother watched his face, wondering what he was thinking. Eventually he said, 'OK, you're right. Let's go there.'

'The Castle?'

'No, Jonathan and April's home.'

They were still wearing their nightclothes as they rushed out of the house. It was a twenty-minute walk to Jonathan and April's, Eleanor's parents', home; Mary's parents ran the whole way. When they got there, Mary's father hammered on the door. A light came on, and moments later, April opened the door a small crack.

'Who is it?'

'It's us. Mary's missing.'

The door opened fully. 'What?'

'Is Jonathan there? We need his help.'

April sighed. 'Jonathan's gone. They all have . . . the Castle Six, I mean . . . they're off on a mission. They're going to the Kingmaker's Castle.'

Mary's mother was getting hysterical. 'Oh God, oh God, what are we going to do?'

April picked up her coat from a peg next to the door. 'It's OK. Don't worry, Diana. We'll go to the Castle. There are people there who can help us.'

The three of them started walking through the community to the castle. Much of the community was in darkness, although there were always a few night owls awake, some with burning torches outside their homes, which was the traditional way of advertising that you wouldn't mind if another lonely insomniac came in for a drink and some nocturnal conversation. When they reached the castle, a night watchman appeared as they made their way through the arched stone doorway and asked them what they were doing there.

'We need to talk to the skeleton staff. A girl's gone missing.'

The night watchman looked concerned. He nodded and went back into the castle's grounds, returning soon after with a red-haired woman. She listened to their story and then told them not to worry.

'This is what I'm going to do,' she explained. 'I'll send two night riders out to explore all the nearby countryside. I'll also send a messenger to catch up with the Castle Six. He'll find them and explain what's happened. You say this girl Mary is a friend of Eleanor's?'

They nodded.

'Don't worry. Everything will be OK. But you must let us handle this the correct way. There's no point getting the whole community into a panic.'

Mary's father held his wife. She leaned against him, still scared, but seeing sense in what the red-haired woman was saying. When she finished talking, they thanked her, and the three of them returned to their homes, destined for a sleepless night.

CHAPTER
THREE

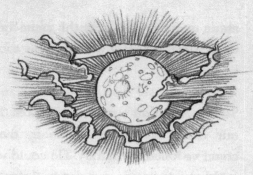

As Anderson carried Mary further into the darkness on the back of his horse, she wondered what to do. He was riding at great speed, with one arm wrapped around her so she couldn't escape. She could bite his hand, but if she tried to jump she'd break her neck. Frustrated, she started screaming and kicking his legs. She did this for a while, but he ignored her. Finally, it seemed to get to him and he slowed the horse, before coming to a complete stop. Turning to face her, he said, 'Mary, what's wrong?'

'Anderson,' she panted, 'please don't kill me.'

He looked amazed, then shocked. 'What are you talking about? Why would I want to kill you?'

'Because you're evil. Eleanor told me.'

Anderson frowned. 'Eleanor said that?'

'Yes. And she told me that she told you I had a crush on you. But it's not true.'

'I didn't come to your house because Eleanor told me

about your crush, Mary. I came because, well, from what Eleanor said, I thought you might be sympathetic to our cause.'

'What cause? You betrayed Eleanor and the Castle Seven. And you supported Basker. He was coming to our castle, to kill everyone in the community! He could've killed my family. He could've killed me.'

'Mary,' Anderson said slowly, 'I don't mean to patronise you, but I don't think you understand about politics. Basker isn't a violent man. We didn't always see eye-to-eye. But he had some extremely important ideas on how to revolutionise the former kingdom. You have to understand that things aren't always as they seem, Mary. A lot of what you've been told is just propaganda.'

Mary wasn't going to be swayed, not without a more convincing explanation of his past behaviour. She said, 'You drew your sword against Eleanor's father.'

'Yes,' he replied, without shame. 'I did, and I kept secrets from everyone. Except Katharine.' Katharine was Anderson's girlfriend, and a former member of the Castle Seven. 'But I did this for a good reason. Mary, I know Eleanor is your friend, and I can see how you might've formed the wrong impression of me. All I can say in my defence . . . and this is something I tried to explain to Eleanor, in my own way . . . is that the Castle Seven – or Six, as I understand they now are – have no idea what they're doing. They just blindly travel about, thinking they're ambassadors, believing they're forming allegiances with people when really they're just eating and drinking and talking about nothing. Our country is changing, Mary, and if we're not careful it could become an extremely dangerous place. The country requires leadership.'

'Are you back with Basker?'

He shook his head. 'That was a temporary alliance. He has good ideas, but Katharine and I believe that more direct action is required. We have new supporters. A new army. An army I think you would be happy to fight alongside.'

'Fight?'

He brushed this aside. 'Just a figure of speech. This is an ideological confrontation.'

'Ideological?' asked Mary, unfamiliar with the word.

'A clash of ideas,' he explained, 'that's all. Now, please get back on the horse. Katharine is waiting for us.'

They were in a dark patch of the wilderness, miles away from any community. Mist rose from the ground, and now they were standing still Mary felt extremely cold. She knew escape was impossible; she had no idea how to get back to her castle. If she was going to survive, she would have to go with Anderson now, and maybe later she could persuade him to return her to the castle. She was frightened about being taken to Katharine: although she had only seen her a few times before and never spoken to her, Eleanor had made her sound even more dangerous than Anderson. But if they had chosen her, they would have to be nice to her.

Wouldn't they?

Chapter Four

Eleanor was the last one down to breakfast. Usually when they were travelling, her father would make sure to wake her up, but this morning, as if he'd known about her troubled night, he'd left her sleeping. She came into the dining-room and took her seat between her father and Sarah. She looked round at the Castle Six and the rest of the children who travelled with them, depressed by how perky everyone seemed this morning. Eleanor knew this was because they were close to the Kingmaker's Castle – if their calculations were correct they might even reach it by late afternoon – and hated being much more tired than everyone else.

Zoran was the one who seemed to enjoy travelling the most. Today he was wearing a pair of dark glasses and his square jaw was shaded with stubble. Although he was younger than Eleanor's father, still in his late twenties, the stubble was flecked with grey and white. He was wearing a fleece he had stripped from a sheep himself and his eyes, as always, were bright with excitement. Alongside Zoran, tucking into a breakfast of bacon and eggs, sat Robert, his younger comrade. Robert had always been in Zoran's shadow, and even his clothes seemed less stylish than his friend's. Eleanor had observed that while Zoran seemed to have grown in confidence since Anderson had left the Castle Seven, Robert had become more cautious. This made him a useful protector, and Eleanor was touched whenever he displayed any kindness to her.

Alexandra, also, had changed since Anderson's departure. She had been the first member of the Castle Seven to truly befriend Eleanor, and had always been a keen organiser of the group's movements. She had known Anderson since she was a child – for a long time the two had been sweethearts – so it wasn't surprising that she had taken the betrayal the hardest. At one time she had always dressed in pinks, oranges and reds. Now she frequently wore black, as Katharine often had. Eleanor wasn't sure if she dressed like this because she was in mourning, or because she wanted to resemble Katharine. She had a very no-nonsense, straightforward relationship with Eleanor's father, and the two of them tended to give most of the orders. Eleanor was pleased that Lucinda remained as light-hearted as ever, her long brown hair wild and untamed, her temperament always good. Eleanor had worried that her adventures wouldn't be as exciting now her father had taken over from Anderson, but she had retained her position as leader of the children, and her father made sure he always gave her plenty of responsibility and never embarrassed her.

Eleanor looked down to the other end of the table, watching Hephzibah as she asked her twin sister Beth, 'Can you pass me the orange juice?'

'I can't reach,' said Beth, although this was clearly untrue.

She scowled, got down from her chair, and went over to pick up the orange juice herself. Hephzibah's relationship with her twin sister had been increasingly troubled for weeks now. This was because both twins had fallen in love with Michael, who was the less immediately attractive of the two boys. Shorter than Stefan, he had been overweight when he first joined the Castle Seven, but the constant riding had left him lean, although he retained his pudgy cheeks. Hephzibah, who was more straightforward than Beth, had hinted to Michael about how she felt about him and the two of them had started behaving romantically towards each other. Eleanor didn't understand why Beth wasn't interested in Stefan. She was also feeling the pangs of frustrated love, having recently been separated from Justin, the first boy she had ever kissed. Eleanor hoped she would see him again one day, and in the meantime she dreamt about him at least three times a week.

She filled a bowl with cornflakes and poured milk on top. Her father grinned at her and she smiled back, beginning to feel more awake.

After breakfast they left the inn and went to the stables where their horses were tied. Eleanor's horse was called Nathaniel and he was grey with a thick, healthy mane. When the rest of the Castle Seven and the children were trapped in the Greengrove Castle's dungeon, Eleanor had escaped on Hephzibah's white steed, a horse she had always coveted. Soon after, Hephzibah had offered her horse to Eleanor, but Eleanor felt loyal to Nathaniel and was reluctant to swap.

Eleanor mounted Nathaniel, and the group rode up the nearby hill. Jonathan and Alexandra usually led the trail, accompanied by Michael and the twins. The two younger men, Robert and Zoran, rode behind them with Stefan. Recently, Sarah, Lucinda and Eleanor had begun to ride at the back of the pack, going slower so they could enjoy a leisurely conversation. Today, Eleanor kept her pace so slow that Lucinda got frustrated and rode ahead, leaving her to enjoy an unobserved exchange with Sarah.

Eleanor yawned. 'I'm so tired.'

Sarah took a moment to respond. 'Couldn't you sleep?'

'I had a nightmare.'

Eleanor knew that Sarah would take this seriously. In the past, her nightmares had revealed hidden dangers that lay ahead, and although Sarah had once been sceptical about the value of Eleanor's nocturnal visions, she had since learnt to respect them.

'About the mission?' she asked.

'No. About home. I think someone's in danger, but I don't know who.'

Sarah considered this. 'I had a troubled night too.'

'Do you think my dream is a message?'

'I don't know, Eleanor. I didn't dream about our community. I dreamt about the Kingmaker's Castle.'

'Do you think it's dangerous for us to go there?'

Sarah laughed. 'No . . . from what I've heard, the people at the Kingmaker's Castle aren't exactly frightening. It's not them I'm worried about, it's what they might know.'

'What d'you mean?'

'Eleanor,' Sarah said seriously, 'what do you know about my background?'

Eleanor wasn't sure how to answer. She wanted to ask her about the Daughters, but it would be impossible to do that without revealing how she had found out that Sarah was connected to them. So instead she said, 'I know that you're the great-great-granddaughter of the last princess before the fall of the kingdom, and the only person in our community who has some knowledge of the way things used to be.'

Sarah looked shocked. 'Who told you that?' Before Eleanor had a chance to answer, Sarah had worked it out herself. 'Alexandra, I suppose. Well, yes, that's true. And do you know why this castle is called the Kingmaker's Castle?'

Eleanor shook her head.

'It's because,' Sarah explained, 'several thousand years ago, it belonged to a man named Richard Neville. He was enormously rich and had a loyal following. Richard Neville was known as the kingmaker because he helped one king obtain his crown and another to return to power. This was thousands of years before my family ruled the country, and many dramatic events have happened in the meantime. But this particular castle, the Kingmaker's Castle – although it has been looted and restored and looted again throughout history – has become a centre for information, and the four people who live there are . . . somewhat separated from their community . . . and spend their time trying to establish the truth about everything that has ever happened in this country.'

'And that's what scares you?'

Sarah looked across at her. 'What scares me is that as soon as they find out about my background, they're either going to question me relentlessly or tell me stuff I don't want to know. It's bad enough that everyone knows about my background. I'm not interested in my past. I've heard the travellers' tales, and read the few books that somehow managed to stay in my family and get passed down to me, but that's it, I don't want to know any more. My life has changed. I am part of the Castle Six now. That's all I care about. All these people who want to restore things to the way they were . . .'

'What people?'

She shook her head. 'It doesn't matter. I shouldn't have told you any of this, Eleanor. Please promise me you won't discuss it with anyone else.'

Eleanor promised. Sarah speeded up and rode away, leaving Eleanor amazed that someone so private had opened up to her, and vowing to herself that she would always keep Sarah's secrets, no matter what.

CHAPTER FIVE

Anderson led his horse into a wild wood. He was going slower now, carefully weaving between the thick trees. Mary felt scared again and asked him, 'Where are we going?'

'We have a shelter here. In the middle of the forest.'

Mary didn't like the sound of this, but thought that if he was going to hurt her, he would've done so already. They had been riding all night, and Mary was exhausted. Occasionally she'd managed to drop off for a short while, before being shaken awake again by the motion of the horse. It was dawn and the forest was full of noise and movement, and Mary held on tightly to Anderson. They travelled deeper and deeper into the forest, eventually stopping by a small stone house.

'Whose home is this?' Mary asked.

'I just told you. It's ours.'

'Yes,' she said, 'but who did it belong to before?'

Anderson turned away. 'It was empty.'

Mary didn't believe him. This wasn't the sort of place anyone would discover accidentally. They must have followed someone here, and kicked him out, or worse.

Anderson dismounted, and helped Mary get down before securing his horse. Kneeling, he looked Mary in the eye and said, in a very serious voice, 'Katharine is under enormous stress at the present time. As long as you're well-behaved, there won't be any trouble, but I warn you that if you make her angry, it could be very dangerous.'

'I thought you said I was safe,' Mary protested.

'You will be, as long as you respect Katharine's will.'

As he said this, Katharine appeared in the doorway. Her jet-black hair was tied back with a thick strand of coarse red material. She was wearing a black dress with thin ribbons of red sewn around the cuffs, collar and hem. She brushed her hand quickly through her hair and said to Anderson, 'So you were successful?'

He laughed and pointed at Mary.

'Did anyone see you?' Katharine asked.

He shook his head. 'Her parents were asleep. It'll be at least another hour before they realise she's missing.'

'What about the Castle Six?'

I spoke to a stable boy. They're away on a mission. To the Kingmaker's Castle.'

Katharine laughed. 'What a great meeting of minds that'll be.'

Anderson didn't respond.

'I've made breakfast. We should eat it and then we can go.'

He shook his head. 'The girl needs to sleep.'

'There's no time. We can't leave Andrew and Stephen in charge any longer. Who knows what they'll have done already.'

'Two hours, Katharine, that's all. The boys won't even be awake yet. If they have done anything terrible, it would've happened last night.'

Anderson and Katharine stared at each other. Eventually, she sighed and stepped back. 'OK,' she said, 'two hours.'

They walked inside the stone house. There was a small wooden table in the centre of the front room. Anderson and Mary sat down and Katharine went out into the kitchen. She returned with two wooden bowls and placed them in front of Anderson and Mary.

'Aren't you eating?' Anderson asked Katharine.

'I've already had mine.'

Mary stirred her food, wondering if it was poisoned. This breakfast wasn't like anything she'd eaten before. A large bowl of gluey green and brown stew, seemingly made out of leaves; an unidentifiable meat; gristle and bones. It tasted bitter but was very filling, and after three mouthfuls Mary wasn't sure whether she could eat any more. Worried that Katharine would be angry if she didn't finish it, Mary struggled for a little while longer and then gave up. Katharine didn't seem bothered, immediately taking the bowl away from her.

The stodgy food made Mary feel sleepy, and Katharine showed her through to the bedroom. Within seconds of lying down, she was asleep.

CHAPTER SIX

Jonathan was a different kind of leader to Anderson. Anderson had always had the stop points carefully worked out, riding towards inns and resting for lunch at approximately the same time every day, usually alongside a stream or some other diversion that would keep the group occupied during their break. He seemed to know every inch of the wilderness, and rarely got lost, unless he was doing so deliberately. Jonathan would take ages finding an interesting spot to eat, often annoying the rest of the Castle Six, especially Zoran and Robert, who would moan about their growling bellies. He was particularly fond of hummocks and knolls, to everyone's bemusement.

Eleanor secured her horse, Nathaniel, and went to join the other children, who had already made a start on the picnic lunches they had purchased at the inn this morning. As she approached them, they immediately fell silent. Anxious, Eleanor asked, 'What were you talking about?'

For a moment no one answered. Then Michael said, in a slow, careful voice, 'The twins are scared. After what happened at the Greengrove Castle.'

Eleanor was relieved. 'No,' she said, 'it won't be like that this time. Sarah told me. She said the people at the Kingmaker's Castle are intellectuals.'

'Inter-what-alls?' Hephzi asked.

'Intellectuals,' Eleanor repeated. 'They're very clever people who are only concerned with the mind. They're great thinkers.'

All the other children were staring at Eleanor. She was usually very careful not to emphasise the fact that she enjoyed a special relationship with the Castle Six, and felt worried that they would think she was showing off because she knew so much about the community they were visiting. She sat down beside Stefan and took out her lunch. He scratched his nose and asked, 'Do you know how many people live in this castle?'

Jonathan overheard them and turned round, saying, 'Only four. In the actual castle, that is. Their community is about as big as ours. There are two men, Stewart and James, and two women, Hedley and Sophie. They're all young, younger than me, even younger than Alexandra and Sarah, I think.'

Eleanor felt grateful to her father for taking over the conversation. He spoke in the same serious way he always had, staring straight at the person who had asked the question. Eleanor's feelings towards her father had changed considerably since he joined the Castle Six. He seemed younger, happier, and much more confident since he had been freed from his job as a handyman in the community, almost a different person. His sandy hair was longer than it used to be, curling over the frayed collar of his shirts (Eleanor had been embarrassed when he had refused the new clothes offered to him by the tailors who worked for the Castle Six) and he often went days without shaving, although never as long as Zoran.

'How much longer will it take us to get there?' Stefan asked.

'Three hours, I think,' he replied. 'We should definitely be there before it gets dark.'

'I hope we have a good meal tonight,' said Robert, who was sitting next to Jonathan.

Jonathan laughed. 'The people at the Kingmaker's Castle aren't exactly known for their hospitality.'

'They must have a chef, though, surely.'

'Yes, but apparently they stick to a very strict diet. Their food is designed to be as bland as possible, so as not to stimulate any unnatural appetites.'

'They sound like weirdos,' said Beth.

Everyone laughed. Beth looked round in shock, surprised to have provoked such a reaction.

'Come now,' said Jonathan, 'wait until you've met them before you form your opinion.'

Beth looked embarrassed. Jonathan smiled and ruffled her hair, saying, 'Although I have to admit you've got a point.'

CHAPTER SEVEN

Mary awoke suddenly, feeling a sharp pain in her shoulder. Katharine was shaking her awake, using far more force than was necessary. Mary felt too scared to complain, and when she opened her eyes Katharine immediately lost interest in hurting her.

'It's time to go,' she told her.

'OK,' said Mary. 'Where's Anderson?'

'Outside. Come on.'

Mary followed Katharine, struggling to keep her eyes open. She felt exhausted, so tired it seemed as if she was sleepwalking. Anderson stood outside with their horses. He put his hands around Mary's waist and lifted her up onto her horse, before sitting in front of her again.

'The girl should ride with me,' Katharine protested.

Anderson ignored her. Mary was glad, knowing the woman would hold her in too tight an embrace. Anderson and Katharine climbed onto their horses and they rode off.

Neither Anderson nor Katharine offered Mary any further explanation of where they were taking her. Anderson had mentioned a 'new army' that she would fight
alongside, and this had excited Mary and frightened
her at the same time. After she'd been chosen by the
Castle Seven, Eleanor had told Mary that part of her
training had been to learn how to sword-fight, although
as far as Mary knew, Eleanor hadn't been called upon
to put these skills into practice. Anderson had been
very specific. She *would* fight. But with a sword?
Against whom? And who would the other soldiers be?

It was several hours before Mary discovered the
answers to these questions. They reached the Kinder
Castle at three o'clock. By this time Mary was so weary
she was almost asleep.

'Kinder Castle?' Mary asked, surprised.

'*Kin-der* Castle,' said Katharine, correcting her pro-
nunciation. 'It means children.'

'There are children here?'

'Oh, yeah.' Katharine smiled. 'You could say that.'

The Kinder Castle was shaped like a giant stone rose. At
the centre of the castle was a squat, round tower with six
semi-circular bastions projecting from its circumference,
and surrounding the bastions was a massive curtain
arranged into six projecting lobes. One of the outer

lobes was higher than the others and contained the entrance, which could only be reached by a drawbridge across the ditch. As they approached, the drawbridge was up.

'Anderson,' Katharine snapped, 'how are we going to get their attention now?'

'Relax,' said Anderson. 'I'll throw a message over the wall.'

'As if they'll notice that. Who knows what's going on inside.'

'Calm down, Katharine. They know we're coming. We're just a bit late, that's all.'

Katharine scowled at Anderson and turned her horse away from him. Anderson dismounted, took a piece of paper from his saddlebag and an ink pen and wrote a short note. He scrabbled around on the ground for a suitably sized rock, then folded up the message and tied it onto the rock with a short length of white string. Leaning backwards, he brought his arm up and tossed the rock high into the sky. It sailed over the outer curtain and into the castle grounds.

'Great,' said Katharine. 'What do we do now?'

'We wait.'

Two minutes later, the drawbridge slowly lowered. As soon as it had come down completely, a girl around Mary's age appeared. She was walking down to welcome them when a fat red tomato landed splat on the side of her head. Mary was shocked, but the girl just laughed and used her fingers to scoop up the red pulp that was dripping down the side of her white neck.

'Where are Andrew and Stephen?' asked Katharine.

'Sleeping,' the girl said. 'I'll take you to them.'

'And what's your name?'

'Naomi,' she said, smiling.

Naomi led them into the large hexagonal bailey at the centre of the castle. Although they kept a safe distance from the action, Mary was still amazed and horrified by what she saw. A scrum of at least three hundred children, all engaged in a giant fruit fight. Everywhere she looked there was a barrel of tomatoes, grapes and other squishy, ripe fruit surrounded by a group of children desperately filling their arms with further ammo. It didn't seem to be a war between particular sides, but rather a game where the only aim seemed to be to get as dirty as possible.

'What on earth is going on?' Katharine demanded.

'Training,' said Naomi casually. 'It was Andrew's idea.'

Anderson laughed. 'Target practice.'

Katharine wasn't amused. 'Did you have anything to do with this?'

'I haven't been here,' Anderson protested. 'You know that.'

'You could have arranged it before we left. Who gave them the fruit?'

'Katharine,' he said in a serious voice, 'I promise you this has got absolutely nothing to do with me.'

Naomi led them up a staircase to the first floor. They continued round the narrow walkway and then stopped outside a large oak door. Naomi knocked.

'We're sleeping,' shouted a petulant voice from inside the room.

'It's Katharine,' she told them.

Seconds later the door opened and Stephen appeared, immediately launching into a fast, wheedling explanation. 'It was all Andrew's fault. He said you wouldn't mind, and even if you did, he didn't care . . . he told me he thinks you . . .'

'Shut up, shut up,' said Andrew, shoving his brother aside. 'It isn't true. Nothing he says is true. He picked all the fruit himself, then made us leave it in the sun until it went rotten.'

'Boys,' Katharine snapped, 'just tell me one thing. Why are you sleeping instead of monitoring the castle?'

'It's too boring,' said Stephen. 'No one listens to us.'

Katharine's voice became even sterner. 'You have to *make* them listen. We put you in charge for a reason. If you can't live up to your responsibilities . . .'

'It's Stephen's fault,' Andrew protested. 'He kept yawning and saying he was tired and he made me start yawning and then I felt tired. I couldn't keep my eyes open, I had to go to sleep.'

'He's lying,' said Stephen. 'I was yawning, but I wasn't tired. It was his idea for us to go to bed.'

Katharine turned to Anderson. 'What do you think? Should we choose two different children to rule the castle?'

Anderson smiled. 'That might not be a bad idea. Maybe we would be better off with girls. Mary, would you like to be in charge?'

Andrew let out an anguished shriek, and then burst into tears. 'No, no, you can't . . . please, please, it's not fair. It's not our fault. We didn't do anything wrong. We didn't, we didn't. All we did was go to sleep.'

Katharine raised her hand, silencing him. 'Is what Stephen said true? Don't you care about pleasing us?'

'No,' he said, 'it's not true. All I want is to make you happy.'

'You want to make me happy?'

'Yes,' said Andrew, in a calmer voice, 'that's what I want.'

'In that case, I want you to stop the children having a fruit fight and make them calm down.'

'OK,' he said, 'I can do that.'

Katharine smiled as Andrew – still in his pyjamas – pushed back the bedroom door and went back out onto the narrow walkway. Mary followed the others as they filed behind him. She felt extremely bemused. The boys' frantic energy startled her, as did their large bodies and exceedingly spiky blond hair. Although she could tell they were younger than her, Mary found it hard to work out their exact age, and had to ask Anderson, who told her, 'They're nine.'

'And why are they in charge?'

He leaned in close to Mary and whispered, 'It was Katharine's idea,' as if this explained everything.

Andrew found a spot where he could be seen by all the fighting children and took out a large blue trumpet. Sounding a single, prolonged note, he waited for the children to notice him. Unfortunately, as soon as they did, their response was to pelt him with rotten fruit. He tried to talk to the children, but the onslaught continued, preventing him from getting a word out. Katharine laughed and pushed him to one side, addressing the gathering herself. 'Yes, I can see you're all enjoying yourselves, but I'm afraid it's time to stop now. If you still have any fruit can you put it back in the barrel, and we'll be down in a minute to start hosing you off.'

The crowd went silent. Mary noticed Anderson had gone from her side, and wondered how he'd got away without her noticing. Katharine was turning back towards them when a single soggy peach sailed up from the throng. It seemed to move in slow motion, and Mary held her breath as the fruit hit the side of Katharine's face, splattering more juice over all of them. The moment this happened Mary heard a loud yelp, not from Katharine, but from someone in the crowd below. She looked over the parapet and saw Anderson clutching the boy who had thrown the fruit, dragging him off by his neck.

'Yes, I'm sure I presented an irresistible target. But if anyone else feels the need to prolong this game, I should warn you that the punishment will be a night in the dungeons.'

This threat seemed to do the trick, and it wasn't long before the crowd had gone.

CHAPTER
EIGHT

The Castle Six were drawing close to the Kingmaker's Castle when they beheld a figure running towards them at tremendous speed. Eleanor noticed her father instinctively reach for his sword, but his hand stopped when the approaching man shouted, 'Don't mind me. I'm just conducting an experiment.'

The man was wearing his clothes back-to-front, so that the buttons on his tartan outfit ran up his back instead of his chest. His dark brown hair was extremely short, little more than a fuzz atop his shiny pate. He stopped suddenly, looked at the large contraption strapped to his wrist and made a note on the clipboard he was carrying. Then he walked back to where the Castle Six had stopped.

'My name's Stewart,' he said, offering his hand. 'I'm sorry about this. I don't think we knew exactly when you were coming. Otherwise we would've organised a proper welcoming committee.'

Stewart had a friendly face, with crinkly lines around his eyes. His eyes seemed almost entirely black, more like a mouse's eyes than a human's. This wasn't the only rodent quality to his features, and Eleanor had a sudden sense that no matter how friendly he seemed, she should be wary of him.

'Have you finished your experiment?' Jonathan asked Stewart. Eleanor could detect a hint of scorn in his voice.

Stewart blinked and looked at his contraption again. 'Well, not really, but I suppose that can do for today. Come on, let me introduce you to the others.'

He turned round and started walking back towards his castle. Eleanor had been so intent on riding that she had only just noticed her surroundings. They were heading towards a large round mound that had the arch of a stone curtain-wall on its left side, with a small gap they could ride through. It seemed an unprepossessing entrance for what was evidently such a large and elaborate castle, and Eleanor wasn't surprised when Stewart turned back and said, 'This is the rear entrance, but we'll take you round to the front later. It's really quite something.'

They followed him inside the castle walls. There was a huge courtyard, with a large circular path surrounding a conical motte. Stewart pointed to the two nearest towers, which were on the left hand side of the courtyard, explaining, 'We each have a tower to ourselves. It's better that way, because we're all very different people, and we need space for all our experiments and studies. I have the best tower. It's on the other side of the castle, to the left of the front wall. It used to belong to James, but he lost it to me in a game of cards.'

'Poker?' asked Zoran eagerly, before adding in a quieter voice, 'I wouldn't mind my own tower.'

'Zoran's tower,' laughed Robert. 'Can you imagine it?'

Zoran looked at his friend, as if uncertain whether to be cross with him. Stewart ignored them both and said in a brisk, breezy voice, 'Oh, we don't play any more. In general, we disapprove of gambling. But at the time James had become very interested in questions of statistics and probability. Needless to say, he was much less interested after I took his tower from him.'

'So who's in those towers?' asked Eleanor.

'Sophie and Hedley. Sophie's in the one nearest us, and Hedley lives in the other one. Let's go over and get them.'

They approached the first tower. It was on the nearest side of an oblong projection, opposite Hedley's tower. The turret was octagonal, and Stewart ran in through the entrance and up the stairs. Moments later, he returned with a woman who, as Jonathan had warned her, was younger than the female members of the Castle Six. Although Eleanor always had trouble judging adults' ages, she thought Sophie might still be a teenager,

perhaps eighteen or nineteen. Her hair was combed into
two thick black plaits, and she was wearing a green dress
that didn't really suit her. Her skin was very pale and
she seemed startled by the sunlight.

'Hello,' she said, 'I'm Sophie.'

The group introduced themselves. When Eleanor
told Sophie her name Sophie came over and clutched
Eleanor's hands in hers. 'When were you born,
Eleanor? Which week?'

'The twentieth.'

'I knew it,' Sophie said happily. 'You're a Quester.
Like me.'

'What's a Quester?'

'It's your birth-sign. Some people used to believe that
the time when someone is born can affect the way they
behave. Hardly anyone in the country believes in the
System any more . . . the ideas are outdated, and all the
people who wrote about it in the first place are dead . . .
and I admit it can seem reductive . . . but if you look at
it with the right sense of detachment . . . it can help you
find out about your past, your future, and most of all,
understanding your inner self. I have guides and charts
I can show you.'

'OK,' said Eleanor.

'Don't be taken in,' Stewart warned her. 'It's a load of
nonsense. But, then again, nonsense is Sophie's special-
ist subject. Oh, it's not harmful, don't you worry. Just

silly superstition. You mustn't take it too seriously, Eleanor, that's all I'm saying. Sophie has spent too much time alone in her tower.'

Sophie ignored Stewart, and helped Eleanor get down from her horse. Two stable boys appeared, and as soon as everyone else had dismounted, the boys took the horses off to secure them. Stewart ran through the entrance of the next tower and went up the stairs. He came back with the third member of the King-maker's Castle's ruling quartet. Her name was Hedley and she was wearing a blue hooded robe over her dark clothes. Her hair was long, blonde and straight. She had blue eyes and a soft, round nose, and even before she'd said anything, Eleanor sensed a self-satisfied air about her.

Stewart took Hedley round the group. She didn't seem that interested in the people she was meeting, although Eleanor realised it probably only seemed that way because Sophie had been so friendly. After she had been introduced to everyone Hedley pulled the hood of her robe over her head and started walking across the courtyard to James's tower. The others followed her.

James's tower was down along the curtain wall from Hedley's. It was taller than the other towers, and pen-tagonal instead of octagonal.

'This tower isn't bad,' said Robert to Stewart.

'It's OK,' he replied, 'but it's nothing compared to mine.'

'How come the men have the nicest towers?' asked Hephzi.

'We were living here first,' said Stewart. 'Hedley and Sophie came later.'

'How did you get to live in the castle?' Stefan asked. 'Do you come from important families?'

Eleanor noticed Sarah looking up hopefully at this question, but Stewart just laughed. 'No, that sort of thing hasn't been important for ages, not in this part of the country, anyway. No, James and I used to live in the Kinder Castle.'

'Really?' asked Alexandra, surprised. 'I didn't know that. What was that like?'

'What's the Kinder Castle?' interrupted Eleanor, before he had chance to answer.

Stewart turned to her and explained, 'It's a castle full of children, Eleanor. No one knows exactly how they got there in the first place, or what happened to their parents, but lots of children started to hear about this place, and they ran away from their communities to go there.'

'Is that what you did?'

Stewart nodded. 'And I really regret it now. I haven't seen my family for eight years, and now I doubt I'll ever get to see them again.'

'Were they horrible to you? Is that why you ran away?'

'No,' he said, 'they were perfectly normal parents. But I was young, and stubborn. I hated doing what I was told, and always thought I knew best. One night we had a silly argument and I packed up my belongings, went round to my best friend James's house, and the two of us ran away. As soon as we got to the Kinder Castle, we realised we'd made a terrible mistake.'

'Why?'

'Because that castle is always in complete chaos. Imagine being able to do exactly what you wanted, all the time. It might sound fun to begin with . . .'

'It *is* fun,' pointed out Zoran.

'But what happens when there's hundreds of children, all doing exactly what they want? The place is full of bullies, and it's actually much worse than being with your family, no matter how horrible they are. No, you five are lucky, especially you, Eleanor. You've got your dad with you, but you still get to have adventures.'

'Why didn't you go home again then?' asked Michael. 'If it was so terrible.'

'Pride,' said Stewart, 'and stupidity. We thought we'd make it work. And in a sense, I suppose we did. We certainly managed to live there for six years, although I still have nightmares about my life there. And then, when we were eighteen and they asked us to leave, instead of going into the wilderness with the other people our age, we decided to explore as much of the country as we possibly could, to try to educate ourselves, to gather information and make up for all the years of schooling we had lost. During our travels, we heard about this place . . . the Kingmaker's Castle . . . and how it had remained empty for hundreds of years, because people believed it was haunted, or cursed, or a breeding ground for disease. When we first came to this castle, James and I were scared, but it turned out all the stories were false, that there was nothing here. Oh, the castle was in a terrible state of disrepair, but nothing that couldn't be fixed.'

'Was there a community here then?' asked Alexandra, in a thoughtful tone.

'Yes,' he replied, 'but they were an extremely superstitious one. Sophie is working on a book about the strange things they used to believe.'

'A book?' asked Eleanor, surprised.

'Well, not a real book, like a Bible or a dictionary. I'm just going to copy out a couple of copies and hand them out to people in the community, so they can find out about themselves. We do that sometimes with other books we have – they're too precious to be touched and very few people in the community can read anyway, but we copy out our own versions for the children and anyone else who wants to read them.'

'And the community don't mind you ruling over them?' Alexandra persisted.

'Well, we don't really rule over them,' said Stewart, bashfully. 'They were so impressed that we came into the castle that they've never challenged us. And they're all too scared to come into the castle's grounds.'

'But what happens when they read Sophie's book?'

'Yeah,' said Stewart to Sophie, 'that's a good point. Maybe you shouldn't write it.'

Chapter Nine

Mary sat in a small antechamber with Anderson and Katharine. Outside the door, there was the tremendous noise of three hundred children stuffing themselves. Walking through to the separate room that had been prepared for them, Mary marvelled at the amazing amounts of sausages and mash piled up on each child's plate. She hadn't been given lunch and was completely starving, barely able to wait for her own meal. So she was even more disappointed when her own dinner turned out not to be sausages, but another bowl of the gluey, bitter stew that Katharine had forced her to eat for breakfast.

'I don't want this,' she said, pushing the bowl away.

'It's good for you,' Katharine replied.

'No,' she protested, 'it's *not* good for you to eat the same food all the time. You're supposed to have a balanced diet.'

Katharine laughed. 'And what would you know about

a balanced diet? I think you'll find that there's all the nutrition you need in this stew.'

'I'm not eating it,' she said, 'I want sausages . . .'

Mary heard the scrape of Katharine's chair, and before Mary even noticed what she was doing, Katharine had her long red hair wrapped around her fist and was about to shove her face into her stew. Mary tried to prepare herself for this, but before it happened, Anderson had leaned across the table and there was the crack of a loud, stinging slap. Katharine let out a shriek and released Mary. Mary looked up, amazed by what was happening.

'You can't treat her like that,' Anderson told Katharine. 'Mary is important to us.'

'She's just a girl,' Katharine replied. 'She should be out there in the dining hall with all the other children. There's nothing special about her.'

'Katharine,' said Anderson, sternly, 'Mary is Eleanor's best friend. She is the key to controlling the Clearheart Community, when that time comes. And, after that, with the right training, she could grow into a leader.'

Mary stared ahead, amazed by what Anderson was saying. She'd been unsurprised when Katharine had said there was nothing special about her, as that was how she usually felt, and why, she was certain that Eleanor had been chosen by the Castle Seven instead of her. She listened carefully to see how Katharine responded, sensing her words were more truthful than Anderson's, and was astonished when she said, 'I'm trying to give her the right training.'

'How? By pushing her face into a plate of food? It's perfectly understandable that she doesn't like the stew. I'm not even sure this diet does all the miraculous things you claim it does.'

'Fine – then why don't you two go and eat sausages with the rest of them?'

Mary looked at Anderson. He nodded towards her and the two of them exited the antechamber and found a space at an empty table. The serving woman who had brought the stew stood near them, waiting for Anderson to give his command.

'Sausages,' he confirmed.

The serving woman nodded and backed away.

'I'm sorry,' Mary said quietly.

Anderson stared at her. 'What for?'

'I don't think Katharine likes me.'

'That's not your fault, Mary. And besides, it's not true.'

Mary snorted. 'Don't try to trick me, Anderson. I believe that you're not a bad person, and I'm grateful to you for taking my side against your girlfriend, but you can't smooth over everything and pretend there aren't any problems here.'

Anderson looked shocked. Mary worried she'd gone

too far, but she was getting so annoyed with the way they were treating her that she felt compelled to speak her mind. After a moment, Anderson's frown turned into a smile.

He said, 'Mary, you are a revelation to me. There is something inside you, a fiery core, that is more powerful than anything Eleanor possesses.'

Mary forced herself not to get excited, remembering what Eleanor had told her about one of the Castle Seven's rules – *If flattered, watch out for an ulterior motive* – and adopting a light tone, replied, 'It's my hair, that's all.'

Anderson laughed. 'What?'

'It's because it's red, isn't it? That's what makes you see me as fiery. I'm not fiery, I'm just a girl. Like Katharine said.'

'Mary, you should know that I'm not really interested in using you to get to Eleanor. I don't care about the Clearheart Community, I simply said that so Katharine wouldn't feel threatened.'

'Why should she feel threatened?'

'Because Katharine has no vision. In some ways, she's as conservative as the Castle Six. All she wants is the security of her own castle . . . the right castle . . . and for everyone to feel afraid of her. Yes, OK, in one way she's right, that is the key to leadership, but it is a temporary leadership, and one that will face dangerous new challenges all the time. I can see ahead of that, to a time when I will probably be dead, and you, Mary, you will rule England.'

Now Mary was certain Anderson was deliberately exaggerating so that she would like him. But why? Did it have something to do with what he said about her being Eleanor's friend? She tried not to get angry about the fact that he was only complimenting her because of who she knew, and felt determined that she would convince him of her worth. She would make herself strong, and worthy of these compliments that currently sounded absurd. Still, it was hard not to be fooled by Anderson's apparent sincerity, and she told herself there was nothing wrong with letting him think she was up to his challenge. She sat there smiling at him and basking in his attention. Even if he was trying to manipulate her, it was exciting enough being treated like an adult, let alone getting all these compliments. The serving woman reappeared with two plates of sausages and mash and a bowl of fresh vegetables. Mary wondered if part of the reason why Anderson was so keen to form a bond with her was because he was lonely. He always talked to Mary as if she was an adult instead of a child, and she knew it must've been hard for him to give up his position in charge of the Castle Seven in return for leading an army of children alongside a woman who seemed to show him scant kindness. Feeling sorry for Anderson, Mary reached out and placed her hand over his. He frowned at her and shook it off, then continued eating his dinner.

Sophie ran into James's tower. They waited. When she returned, she was alone.

'He says he's in the middle of something and can't be interrupted.'

'Oh, that's ridiculous,' said Stewart. 'Let me go up and get him.'

'He knew you'd say that,' Sophie told Stewart, 'and he said to let you know he's very close to making a discovery.'

'Really? What's he working on?'

'Magic squares.'

'Magic?' asked Stefan, his voice excited.

'Not that sort of magic,' Stewart explained. He took a piece of parchment from his pocket and drew a 3x3 grid on it. In the first three boxes he wrote the numbers 4, 9 and 2. Beneath this he added 3, 5 and 7. Then, in the bottom three squares he wrote 8, 1 and 6. 'Now,' he said, 'this is the simplest magic square. It was first discovered thousands of years ago in a land very far away from here. No matter what line you choose, every horizontal or vertical row of figures always adds up to fifteen. There are different permutations of numbers that can be used, or if you prefer, you can use words or names instead. It's a puzzle or a game that many people believe has cosmic significance, and has intrigued many great thinkers over the years . . . although I hasten to add that James is not a great thinker, and I very much doubt his discovery is as important as he thinks it is. Nevertheless, if he wants to be left alone, we shall obey his wishes. You'll meet him at dinner. Now, if the women would like to follow Hedley and Sophie and the men come with me.'

The group divided and Eleanor walked alongside Sophie and Sarah.

'So,' asked Eleanor, 'when did you and Hedley come to this castle?'

'Two years ago,' said Sophie, without hesitation. 'Before that we were at the Sisters' Castle. Do you know where that is?'

Eleanor felt her chest tighten. 'Is it anything to do with the Daughters' Castle?'

Sarah looked shocked. 'How do you know about the Daughters' Castle?'

'I heard my mum mention it once,' Eleanor lied.

'Your mum?' Sarah was puzzled. 'How would she know about it?'

Eleanor thought quickly. 'I don't think she knows much about it. I just asked her about the other castles once. The names of them, I mean, and she mentioned the Daughters' Castle.'

'But no one in our community knows about the other castles. Unless . . . did she know Anderson? Before he formed the Castle Seven, I mean?'

'I don't think so. But my Dad . . . Jonathan . . . well, as you know, he used to go out beyond the limits of our community.'

'I didn't know that. Oh, OK, I see. Anyway, it doesn't matter.'

Eleanor noticed that Sophie was looking at Sarah with suspicion. But Sarah's expression was inscrutable, and as they continued walking, Sophie said, 'Yes, Eleanor, to answer your question, it is something to do with the Daughters' Castle. The Daughters' Castle is a castle for any women who have a connection with the last royal family before the fall of the kingdom, as well as their husbands and their offspring. Many people believe the Daughters' Castle is an evil place, and the Sisters' Castle stands in deliberate opposition to it, offering a refuge for women who do not have any connections to illustrious families. The Sisters believe that intellect is just as important as someone's birthright.'

'Do you believe the Daughters' Castle is an evil place?' Sarah asked Sophie.

Eleanor watched as the two women stared at each other. Had Sophie guessed that Sarah had a connection to the Daughters' Castle?

'No,' Sophie said eventually, 'but I do believe that if a castle is so interested in hiding their secrets, they're probably up to something bad.'

'What about the Kingmaker's Castle? Don't you have secrets?'

'We have information here, yes, but it's not secret. We keep it from the community to protect them, and because we believe it's only through studying this information that we can make new discoveries. Discoveries that can help the whole community, maybe the whole country.'

'Don't you think that might be true of the Daughters' community too?'

Sophie laughed.

'What's so funny?' Sarah asked. Eleanor could tell she was really annoyed.

'I'm sorry,' she said, 'I don't mean to laugh. But I don't think anyone believes that the Daughters' Castle is interested in benefiting mankind. They're more concerned with trying to make themselves look beautiful and reminiscing about how the world used to be . . . back in the good old days.'

Sarah seemed about to say something, then shook her head and bit her lip. The group of women and girls came together in front of the extraordinarily large cluster of buildings where they would be staying. There were twelve separate buildings that Eleanor could see, with several more set back behind them. One of the buildings was almost as big as the entire Clearheart Castle. Hephzi pointed at a nearby tower. 'Is that tower empty?'

'Yes,' said Sophie. 'in fact, there are two unoccupied towers here. But only one that's habitable. The other is our spy tower. Not that we have much need of that any more.'

'Can I stay in it?' Hephzi asked excitedly. 'The normal tower, I mean. Not the spy one.'

'No,' shouted Beth before Sophie had chance to answer. 'Why should she get to stay in the tower? It's not fair.'

Alexandra gave Sophie an imploring look. 'Is the spy tower really uninhabitable?'

Sophie seemed to understand the problem, but still said, 'There isn't a bed up there.'

'She wouldn't need a bed. Just some bedding and she could sleep on the floor.'

'I don't want to sleep on the floor,' protested Beth.

'*I* don't mind,' said Hephzibah quickly. 'I'll sleep on the floor if it means I get to stay in a tower.'

The adults exchanged a longer look and then Sophie said, 'OK, we'll find some bedding for you. The rest of you follow me.'

Hephzibah and Beth, both of whom now seemed happy, disappeared into their towers, while the others walked across to a small entrance that led through to a short stairway. At the bottom of the stairway was a huge hall. Sophie looked at Sarah and Alexandra, pleased they seemed to be impressed.

'Would you like to be in the red bedroom or the green bedroom?' Sophie asked Eleanor.

'Are there only two bedrooms?' Eleanor replied, worried. 'Will I have to share?' Sophie laughed. 'No, of course not. And even if you did, these rooms are so big you'd barely notice the other person. But, no, I simply assumed that Alexandra and Sarah would want to stay in the Cedar bedrooms.'

Eleanor looked round. She could tell everyone was confused by Sophie's suggestions, all eager to get a good bedroom but not wanting to seem as childish as the twins. Eleanor decided to leave the decision to Lucinda.

'I don't mind,' she told her, 'you can choose.'

'Is there a pink bedroom?' Lucinda asked, smiling.

'One of the Cedar bedrooms is pink.'

'You can have that room,' said Alexandra to Lucinda, 'I'd prefer the red room.'

'OK,' said Eleanor, 'I'll go in the green room.'

'Good,' said Sophie, 'let me show you.'

CHAPTER
ELEVEN

Sophie hadn't exaggerated. Eleanor's bedroom was magnificent. Any feelings of envy she might have had about not getting her own tower completely disappeared, and she worried one of the twins might see her huge bed and want to swap. It was always a relief to get to a castle after days of travelling, but Eleanor had never felt quite so pleased to be somewhere. Her room was designed to look like a wooden grove which was disconcerting given how much time she had spent in the countryside for real, but there was a major difference between sleeping on the floor and on a soft bed. She took off her muddy boots and rubbed her feet, before stretching out and letting the mattress take the weight of her body. It was heavenly, but dangerous. She was supposed to be getting ready for their evening meal and knew that if she lay there for a moment longer she would fall asleep.

Eleanor stood up and looked at the large leather bag

on her bedroom floor. Packed inside the bag were all the outfits the tailor had made for her when she had first been chosen to join this group. Eleanor always wore a blue dress for riding and travelling (the tailor had made her a second version of this dress after the first had become worn out through heavy use), keeping the others for when she arrived at a castle. Tonight she decided to wear the silver dress. It was her favourite, although she'd recently realised that the long conical hat the tailor had made her to go with it was too ostentatious. Ready for the evening ahead, she put her boots back on and went in search of the others.

Alexandra and Sarah were waiting in the courtyard. The sun was setting and Eleanor felt a sudden wave of excitement. She was enjoying being at the Kingmaker's Castle much more than the Greengrove Castle, and was looking forward to the night ahead. Since Katharine and Anderson had left the Castle Seven the group had grown a lot more relaxed about social occasions. In their initial training the group had been advised to treat conversations as an intellectual battlefield, which made sense when you were dealing with someone as sinister as Basker, but it was clear that the four denizens of the Kingmaker's Castle were interested in fostering an atmosphere of education and enlightenment and there was no reason for adopting such a suspicious attitude here.

Eleanor walked over to the two women. She was still

occasionally surprised by their beauty, especially the contrast between their travelling clothes and the way they dressed when keen to impress. Eleanor even felt a little intimidated by their elegance, and was relieved when Lucinda appeared. It wasn't that Lucinda was any less beautiful, just that her femininity had a friendlier quality. When Alexandra and Sarah dressed up, they seemed keen to separate themselves from the children, whereas Lucinda's wild, untamed hair and irresistibly friendly face meant that Eleanor always felt comfortable with her. Eleanor didn't like to think too much about the Castle Six's romantic inclinations, but she sensed that tonight Alexandra and Sarah wanted to talk to the men, while Lucinda wanted to have fun.

The twins came down from their towers, and Sophie reappeared to tell them they would be having their dinner in the dining-room adjacent to the main hall. In the distance, Eleanor could see the boys and men coming from their accommodation, and Alexandra asked Sophie, 'Will James be joining us for dinner?'

'Yes,' she replied, 'I had a quiet word with him.'

Eleanor remembered what her father had said about how the inhabitants of the Kingmaker's Castle had a very strange diet and worried about what she would be served. In her training she had been taught not to complain no matter what was put in front of her (one time, as a joke, Zoran had instructed the Clearheart Castle's chef to serve them a bowl of worms), but Eleanor had plain tastes and felt scared that the food might be too exotic for her. But the first course was a simple soup and she relaxed, realising she had no reason to worry.

James was a thin man with a large nose and curly brown hair. He wore a black cloak that was too big for him and he had to keep pushing up his sleeves to stop them trailing in his food. Eleanor felt an immediate fondness for this man and listened in as Alexandra asked him questions about his work.

'So,' she asked, 'did you make a discovery?'

James stared out into the dark fringes of the hall. He seemed to wait for ages before saying with a sigh, 'No, not today.'

'Because we interrupted you?'

'Well,' he said, spooning soup into his mouth, 'that didn't help. But, no, that wasn't the main reason. The problem with true intellectual exploration, Eleanor, is that much of your activity will inevitably prove fruitless. There was a period . . . long ago . . . when every new discovery would lead, in time, to the next discovery . . . but so much has been lost that most of our work is going over what we already know and looking for the stuff that fills the gaps and hoping that you'll make the small discovery that illuminates the whole. The best way of explaining it is . . . do you know what fairy lights are?'

Eleanor shook her head.

'Don't worry,' he said, 'I didn't expect you would. There was a time when Christmas was a very different sort of celebration than it is now. It used to be more about money, and ostentatious display, and part of this was about decorated trees . . .' Eleanor laughed. James smiled. 'I know, it is funny. These wouldn't be trees in the forest, but trees that people had cut down, or had had cut down, and taken into their homes. And they would decorate these trees, and one of the things that every Christmas tree would have is fairy lights. Fairy lights were a string of little lights, in lots of different colours; red and yellow and blue and green, and they were pretty, but they had one terrible flaw. If one of the lights was broken, or slightly unscrewed, the whole string would go out and you'd have to check the bulbs one by one. And that's what intellectual endeavour is like today, you have a string of fairy lights that don't work and you have to test each one, hoping that you'll be able to make the whole lot light up again.'

A servant appeared and cleared away the empty soup bowls from the table. Eleanor tried to think of something to say to James. He was staring at her expectantly, but her mind was blank. Fortunately, he was soon distracted by the second course. It was a large bowl of gluey green and brown stew – unbeknownst to Eleanor, exactly the same sort of food that her friend

Mary had recently rejected, in a very different castle, in favour of sausages. James noticed Eleanor frowning and said, 'Oh, don't be scared, Eleanor. This stew is very good for you. It's something they eat at all the most advanced castles.'

This interested Eleanor. 'Have you been to *all* the other castles?'

He shook his head. 'No, I don't really enjoy travelling. They say it broadens the mind, but I find it narrows mine. In fact, I think I've only been to about seven other castles. But lots of visitors from other castles come here, and there are other forms of contact.'

'Like what?'

'Oh, you know, stories, recipes, travellers' tales . . . that sort of thing.'

Eleanor nodded and took a spoonful of stew. It was so bitter that it made her gag and she had to struggle not to spit it out. She looked round at the twins, and Michael and Stefan, and Zoran and her father, certain one of them would make a face of complaint, but everyone else was cheerfully eating their food without comment. Feeling embarrassed, she swallowed the stew and took another mouthful.

After dinner, Jonathan stood up with a glass of wine and announced to the group, 'I'm sorry to interrupt, but on behalf of the Castle Six and the members of the

Clearheart community, I would like to make a toast.'

Everyone looked at him.

'When I was asked to join the Castle Six, I had no real understanding of what my duties might entail. I knew they were good people, because they had chosen my daughter Eleanor to travel with them, but although there was a time when I had roamed freely through the country, the notion of trying to maintain civil order through communication . . .' He laughed and shook his head. 'Well, that sounded like a burden I was uncertain whether I'd be able to handle.

'But if I'd have known that being a member of the Castle Six would lead to wonderful evenings such as this one, I wouldn't have had a moment's doubt. As we all know, this is a turbulent time for our country. Until recently, I had no real understanding of what that meant. I am a humble man, with low ambitions, and all I wanted to do was prosper within my community. And I believe that most people in England are just like I used to be. But if they knew our freedom is a luxury that could soon be under attack, they would want to know what they could do about it. And it is up to us, as representatives of our communities, not to see ourselves as privileged, but as serving the greater good, in the best way we can. Tonight should be a celebration of our future, and I would like you all to raise your glasses to a time when our country is reunited.'

Everyone toasted. Then Sophie said, 'Good. Now, if you'd like to take your seats by the stage, it's time for this evening's entertainment.'

CHAPTER TWELVE

Even before they had taken their seats, there was a flash of smoke and two strangers appeared on the makeshift stage. The man was wearing an old-fashioned tweed suit. Eleanor had seen people dressed like this in photographs and paintings, but never before in real life. He had a shock of white hair and a clown's red nose. The woman was wearing a skin-tight blue costume and a large yellow wig.

Eleanor looked round at the faces of her friends. Everyone seemed as awestruck as she felt, and she caught Alexandra's eye and giggled.

The man said, 'Welcome, we are Cable and Miggs, the most famous storytellers in the whole of England. We have a repertoire that stretches back thousands of years into the past, and many of our stories can be shaped and changed to fit your precise requirements. But tonight's story is a traditional piece, one we can only tell on certain special evenings, due to a specific requirement that you fulfil.'

Eleanor noticed the woman, Miggs, going into the audience and taking Hephzibah and Beth by the hand. Both twins seemed really excited and pleased to be taking part in the action.

'This is the story of a woman called Helena, and a man named Martin. Helena was a very beautiful woman, who fell in love with Martin when they were both eighteen.'

Miggs handed Hephzibah a mask. The mask showed a beautifully made-up woman's face. Hephzibah held this face over her own, and after Miggs had given her a gentle nudge, walked out onto the stage. Then Miggs returned into the audience and pulled out Stefan. Eleanor could tell he didn't want to go with Miggs, but also that he felt duty-bound to be a good sport. Miggs gave Stefan a second mask, this one showing an angry man's face.

'Martin was well-known in his community. He was considered to be a very fierce man, who had enormous trouble controlling his temper.'

Miggs whispered something into Stefan's ear, and he started strutting up and down the stage, growling and shaking his fist. She ducked back into the audience and dragged up Jonathan and Alexandra, giving them both masks with blank expressions. Eleanor was amused to see her father being forced to take part, and felt pleased that he was so relaxed about it. Before he had joined the

Castle Six he would never have done something like this, and it reminded her how far they had come.

'But when Helena's parents tried to warn their daughter about her boyfriend, she refused to listen to them.' Hephzibah put her hands over her ears.

Cable carried a small table to the centre of the stage. Stefan sat behind it. Cable placed a large plate of food on the table and handed Stefan a large stick.

'They told her Martin ate chitterlings all day long. Does everyone know what chitterlings are?'

'No,' shouted Eleanor.

'The small intestines of pigs,' said Cable.

'Ugh,' chorused several of the audience.

'They also said that he had a big stick that he used to beat children, and that he was infamous for getting into fights at the local tavern, but no matter what they said, Helena stood by her choice of boyfriend. Martin was her man, and she would marry him.

'On the night before the ceremony, her parents decided they could stand by no longer and something had to be done. Her mother . . .' Miggs nudged Alexandra forwards '. . . sneaked into Helena's bedroom in the middle of the night and plucked three hairs from her daughter's head. Then they locked her in the dungeon of their community's castle.'

Hephzibah held up a wooden square with three bars in front of her masked face.

'Helena's parents took these three hairs to the Scientist.' Miggs pulled James up on stage. He looked a bit startled, but then Miggs gave him a white coat, a mask and some scientific instruments and he seemed to calm down. 'And the Scientist used them to create a perfect clone of Hephzibah.' Beth walked onto the stage. 'She was identical to Helena, and the following morning, it was this new, counterfeit wife who went to marry Martin.'

Miggs pulled Sarah and Lucinda onto the stage. They were both laughing, and she got the two of them to join hands and hold their arms aloft to symbolise, Eleanor immediately recognised, a church steeple. They hummed a wedding march and Stefan and Beth ran beneath their arms. Miggs reached into a clay pot and threw confetti and rice over their heads.

'The ceremony was a great success,' Cable continued, 'and afterwards, there was a huge party. Everyone in the community attended this celebration. And among the revellers at the wedding reception, there was one man who loved Helena even more than Martin.' Miggs pulled Michael from the audience. Cable's voice took on a more serious tone. 'Peter had been in love with Helena ever since they were children. He was an extremely shy man, and had previously never felt confident enough to voice his love. But on the day that Helena married he decided he could keep his secret no longer. His biggest fear had always been that Helena would reject him, and today he realised that no longer mattered. If she rejected him it would be because she was now a married woman. But if she gave him any sign that she felt the same way, he would beg her to forget about Martin and run away with him.

'Although the counterfeit Helena was physically identical to the real one, she had a mind of her own, and when Peter approached her with his declarations of love, she found him so attractive and kind that she greeted him with a happy response. Soon the two of them spent every day strolling through the nearby countryside . . .'

Michael and Beth walked across the stage together holding hands.

'And, of course, it was only a matter of time before Martin found out. He was so angry that, in a fit of rage, he strangled Helena until she was dead.'

Stefan pretended to do this. Beth fell to the floor. Michael gave a large fake scream.

'Peter was so angry and upset that although he was physically much weaker than Martin, he summoned up all his strength and beat him to the ground.'

The two boys had a comical stage-fight, which prompted everyone in the audience to ignore the disturbing nature of the story and start laughing. Michael held Stefan by his collar and pulled his fist back.

'But before he could deliver that final, fatal blow, the Scientist appeared with the real Helena and her parents.

They had been watching everything and the real Helena was horrified to see that her parents had been right about Martin. The fake Helena turned to dust before their eyes . . .' There was another stage-explosion and Beth disappeared. 'And Martin couldn't believe what was happening. He shouted and protested and fought and cried, but the Scientist still managed to fit handcuffs around his wrists and he was taken to the community's prison.'

James led Stefan away.

'Helena told Peter she had no idea that he had such feelings for her, and although she had to confess that she had never considered him as a possible husband before, she was touched by his emotion and willingness to wait to see if a romance could develop between them. This was more than Peter had ever hoped for, especially after believing that he had just witnessed his beloved's murder, and he agreed to give her time. Helena's parents were satisfied Peter was a man of honour, and eternally grateful to the Scientist for saving their daughter from Martin. And several months late . . .' Miggs got Sarah and Lucinda to recreate their church steeple '. . . the community witnessed another marriage, only this time everyone knew it would end happily ever after.'

Eleanor clapped her hands as loud as she could, wowed by the story. Cable and Miggs gathered their chosen performers into a line, and prompted them to take a bow. They did so, and everyone swapped smiles, delighted by the evening's entertainment. When the applause died down, Eleanor asked, 'Where's Beth?'

'I'm here,' she said, emerging from behind a curtain.

Everyone applauded again, and the two sisters embraced. Eleanor's heart rose, thinking that after all their recent bickering, the conflict between Hephzibah and Beth had finally come to an end. Unfortunately, as Eleanor would soon discover, no matter how relieved Hephzibah seemed that her sister hadn't disappeared for real, this was far from the case.

Chapter Thirteen

Katharine had decided not to join them for the evening's manoeuvres. She was staying back at the Kinder Castle while Anderson led an army made up of the most committed children out into the countryside. When they attacked a castle every child would take part, but most of them would be foot soldiers, there to overpower by number if they failed by force. The fifty children assembled here this evening would be armed and placed at the front of the attack. The large brothers, Andrew and Stephen, stood with Mary, watching as Anderson walked down the line of children, giving each of them a large leather bag filled with stones. He showed them how to strap the bag to their belts, and told them they should always try to keep the bag full, and to keep an eye out for good stones when they were travelling. When he came to Mary, she was surprised to find him thrusting a bag into her hands too.

'I don't want one,' she said.

'Don't be silly, Mary. You, Andrew and Stephen will fight with the others. Don't worry, you won't be at the front, but you'll be in the second rank, and you'll need to attack as well as defending yourselves.'

'Yeah,' said Stephen, 'it's going to be cool.'

When everyone had attached their bag of stones to their belt, Anderson walked down the line again, handing out slingshots and crossbows that had been modified to fire stones instead of arrows.

'Now,' said Anderson, 'in the right hands, with the right training, these could be deadly weapons. But that is not what I want from you. In fact, I want you to take the utmost caution not to kill or maim your targets. We have many advantages over the Baldwin Castle, not least that this will be a surprise attack, and it should be possible to overwhelm our enemy and take their castle for our own with a minimum of force. Fear is our primary weapon, and the point of this training is to make our army as terrifying as possible.'

Anderson pointed to a copse in the near distance. 'For tonight's purpose, those trees will serve as the Baldwin Castle. Your aim is to hit as many trees as possible with stones and to scream and charge towards them as if they were a human army. I have painted eyes and other body parts you should try to avoid hitting onto the tree trunks. There is no way of scoring points and I'm not looking to evaluate individual performance. The point of this exercise is to see how well you work as a team . . . as an army. OK? Take your positions. You too, Mary . . . join Andrew and Stephen at the back.'

Mary did so. The children were all crouching down, waiting for the order to attack. It was clear they had already undergone weeks of training, and Mary felt determined not to seem weak or nervous alongside them. More than anything, she wanted Anderson to continue to admire her. Mary knew Eleanor would disapprove of her behaviour, but how different was it to what she had done when she joined the Castle Seven? She must've believed Anderson once, and he claimed he still had the same aims he'd had then, just a different way of achieving them. And besides, she thought angrily, why did she care so much about what Eleanor thought? Her friend had abandoned her without a second thought, and the possibility of getting one back at her was thrilling.

'ATTACK!' screamed Anderson, and Mary found herself charging forward, caught up in the incredible excitement of this fake battle. She had to be careful not to hit the heads of the children in front of her and aimed her crossbow high, still making sure that she kept the tree targets in sight. It was hard to tell how many of her stones hit home in the hail, but she believed Anderson would be able to tell, even in the near-darkness.

The assault continued for five minutes, then Anderson gave the order for them to stop. A column of children toppled and Mary fell sideways, landing in the wet grass.

'Thank you, children,' Anderson said with a smile. 'That was excellent.'

CHAPTER FOURTEEN

Everyone agreed the storytellers had been an incredible success. Even Hedley, who claimed Cable and Miggs's story was merely a modern variation on a Euripides play she had in her personal library, had to admit that the performance had been delivered with panache. The entertainment was the highlight of the evening, and although the adults clearly enjoyed the wine and conversation that followed, Eleanor soon began to feel bored and she was relieved when everyone retired to bed at ten o'clock.

Alone in her bedroom, Eleanor was just about to change into her nightgown when there was a knock at the door. Eleanor thought she knew who it was. Although Michael was supposed to be in love with Hephzibah, and Eleanor believed he genuinely did have those feelings for her, for some reason he liked to get Eleanor to join him on the occasional night adventure.

Usually this happened when they were travelling – like the time when he sneaked into her room through a secret entrance hidden inside a wooden man when they were on their way to the Greengrove Castle – but maybe tonight he would want her to join him while they explored their new surroundings.

'Hello, Michael,' she said, as she opened the door.

But it wasn't Michael. It was Beth, and she had tears in her eyes.

'Beth,' said Eleanor, 'what's wrong?'

She rubbed her eyes. 'Will you come up to my tower with me?'

'Of course. What's the matter?'

Beth didn't reply, instead turning round and walking through the hall to the stairs and courtyard. Eleanor quickly put her boots back on and followed her. It was cold outside and Eleanor's arms prickled. She wished she had time to go back inside and put a cardigan on over her dress, but Beth was clearly in no mood for delay. She wondered what could have happened in the short time since they'd gone to their beds.

Beth went through the doorway to her tower. Eleanor followed closely behind. There were candles set into small grooves in the stone walls, illuminating the spiral staircase that ran up to the bedroom at the top of the tower. When they reached the bedroom, Beth flung herself face down on the mattress. Eleanor sat down and listened as Beth said, 'She's a total cow. I hate her so much.'

'Who?'

She rolled over and made a face, as if the answer was obvious and Eleanor was being stupid.

'My sister, of course. Who else?'

'Oh,' said Eleanor, feeling relieved, 'what's she done now?'

'She doesn't have to do anything to be annoying, she just is. But the reason she's made me cross tonight . . . Eleanor, if I tell you something secret, do you promise not to tell anyone?'

Eleanor had to think before answering this question. She remembered her promise to Alexandra when she'd first joined this group to tell her if any of the children were unhappy, and realised this was exactly the sort of situation she meant. But Beth's feelings for Michael were hardly secret, and it seemed unlikely that whatever Beth told her was going to be that surprising, so after a brief hesitation, she said, 'Yes, of course.'

'I'm fairly certain that Michael likes me a lot more than Hephzibah, and he's only going out with her because she told him how she felt first.'

'Has he told you this?'

Beth shook her head. 'But he doesn't need to. When we were acting out that story, and he held my hand, I could just tell.'

'Have you said anything to him?'

'No. How could I? Hephzibah would never speak to me again. But if the decision came from him, if he told her, then it would be different. She couldn't blame me then, no matter how upset she was.'

Beth looked at Eleanor with eager eyes, waiting for her response. Eleanor found herself thinking about how she had never muddled up the twins. There was a physical difference between them, but it was incredibly slight. Beth was fractionally smaller than Hephzibah, with a bigger nose and shorter brown hair, but even if Eleanor only caught a brief glimpse of one of the twins from behind, she immediately knew who it was. Hephzibah was both calmer and more confident than her sibling, while Beth was a ball of nervous energy.

'So,' said Eleanor, 'you want Michael to decide for himself that he likes you more than your sister?'

'He's already decided,' Beth protested. 'But he's scared. I need you to hint to him that it will be all right with everyone if he ditches Hephzibah and starts going out with me.'

Eleanor stared at Beth, flabbergasted. 'I can't do that.'

'Why not? You're my friend, aren't you?'

'Yes, of course, but I'm Hephzibah's friend too.'

'You prefer her to me.'

'No. Listen, Beth, that's not it. But I can't interfere in your sister's relationship.'

'I'm not asking you to. Just talk to him. Find out how he feels. And when he mentions me, just say . . . it'll be OK, everyone will understand.'

Beth seemed so hopeful that this was the ideal solution that Eleanor couldn't bring herself to refuse outright, and instead said, in a cautious voice, 'I could talk to him, but I'm not going to encourage him to go out with you.'

'No, that's OK, you don't have to. Just encourage him to confide in you, and then tell me what he says.'

Eleanor frowned. 'I can't promise anything, Beth.'

'You don't have to,' she replied, 'I trust you, El.'

Chapter Fifteen

Mary was awoken by a knock at her bedroom door. Worried it might be one of the twin, she burrowed under her covers, waiting for them to go away. But then there were several louder knocks and Mary realised it was an adult outside her door.

She got out of bed and went to open the door. It was Anderson, still dressed in muddy battle-clothes from the night exercises.

Mary rubbed her eyes. 'Is something wrong?'

'No,' he replied. 'Can I come in?'

She stood back and let him inside. He gestured for her to get back into bed and then took a seat by the single window in her dark bedroom.

'You did well tonight,' he told her. 'Especially without any training. My observations were definitely correct. You are extremely promising, Mary.'

She blushed. 'Thank you, Anderson.'

'The best way to thank me is to exploit your talents to the fullest. When I think of how close you came to living an ordinary life, of never discovering your gifts, of being damned to spend your days trapped with your boring family . . .'

Mary felt hurt. 'I love my family.'

'But you must have always known that you were smarter than them, that you didn't belong. It's OK, Mary, it's nothing to be ashamed of. And I'm not trying to make you big-headed either. It's just a fact of life. Some people are born special. You're one of them. The fact the Castle Seven didn't notice you when they were observing Eleanor, well, that kind of oversight just shows how irrelevant they are.'

Mary tried to fight a yawn, but was so sleepy she couldn't stop it escaping.

'You're tired,' Anderson observed. 'I'm sorry; I shouldn't be keeping you up. Don't worry – tomorrow shouldn't be too strenuous. But, nevertheless, I should let you go to bed.'

'Thanks, Anderson,' she replied.

'Goodnight, Mary. Pleasant dreams.'

CHAPTER SIXTEEN

Eleanor was still feeling deeply agitated as she left her tower and walked back to her room. It didn't help when she spotted Michael, who was waiting outside her door.

'Where have you been?' he asked.

'Talking to Beth. Why? What business is it of yours?'

'None,' he replied, 'I'm sorry, I just thought you might like to go on a little exploration trip.'

'Michael,' she said, in a serious voice, 'why don't you go exploring with Hephzibah instead of me? She *is* your girlfriend.'

'Because it's more fun with you. Besides, I know that you sometimes have trouble sleeping. Like me.'

This seemed a satisfactory answer, and Eleanor felt embarrassed about being sharp with him. She supposed she was really still angry with Beth, and was taking it out on the object of her affection. Why did everything have to be so complicated? Stefan was a perfectly pleasant boy; surely Beth could be his girlfriend instead? Then everything would be fine.

'Yeah,' she said, 'I like exploring with you too, Michael. I'm sorry for being grumpy. Maybe I'm tired.'

'We don't have to explore tonight. If you want to go to bed.'

'No,' she said, 'it's OK. Where do you want to go?'

'I don't know. I thought we could just walk around the grounds.'

'OK,' she said, 'but let me just get a cardigan from my room. My arms are cold.'

'Of course.'

She went back into the green room and picked up a blue cardigan. She put it on and rejoined Michael. They went back out into the courtyard and walked slowly together.

Eleanor asked, 'Do you like this castle?'

He smiled. 'Very much. You?'

'Yes, I like it too. Especially the people. James and Sophie.'

'Hedley seems a bit grumpy, doesn't she?'

'Yes. But it's a different type of grumpiness to someone like Anderson. It's not frightening. What I mean is, you know you can trust her.'

'I agree. I don't know why we didn't come to this castle first. It would've been a much safer place to start.'

Their boots crunched against the gravel. Eleanor

pointed at the castle mound and the exit in the centre of the rear wall. 'Shall we go out beyond the mound?'

'Yes,' said Michael, 'then maybe we could walk round the perimeter wall for a bit. See what we find.'

Eleanor smiled at Michael, pleased that he had the same thoughts as her. They walked together, not saying anything for a short distance, and then Eleanor asked, 'Did you enjoy taking part in the story tonight?'

Michael gave her a sideways glance.

'Yes,' he said. 'Did Beth?'

'What makes you ask that?'

'I thought you might've been talking about it with her.'

The way Michael looked at Eleanor made her suspicious. Why was he asking this question? Did he suspect something? The worst possibility was that he knew how Beth felt and was toying with her. Surely he wouldn't be that cruel?

'No,' said Eleanor, 'she didn't mention it.'

Michael stared at her. Eleanor was amazed at how much more confident he had become. It was strange for all of them, being children in a more prominent position (and having better lives) than most of the adults in the community, but the idea that this might affect the way they interacted with each other disturbed her. The romantic tensions currently emerging seemed as if they would be hard enough to handle without Michael becoming arrogant. She thought back to when they'd first been chosen, and how disappointed she'd been when she first saw Michael. Although it wasn't that long ago – barely three months – he had changed completely in this time. No longer overweight, his pudgy cheeks were the only evidence of the shy boy he used to be.

'Yes,' he said, in answer to her question, 'I did enjoy the acting. It was fun. Hephzi enjoyed it too.'

Eleanor nodded. They reached the castle mound and walked through the exit. Michael pointed into the darkness.

'Look, there's someone there.'

'Where?' asked Eleanor.

'There. Coming towards us.'

Scared, Eleanor reached for Michael's hand. He took it, but asked, in an impatient tone, 'What's wrong?'

'We might get in trouble. It could be a night watchman.'

'It's not a night watchman.' He squinted into the darkness. 'It's . . . your father, and who's that with him?'

Eleanor strained her eyes. It was Alexandra, walking alongside her father. Seeing these two together shocked her, but they didn't seem to mind being spotted. Jonathan waved at her, and she heard Alexandra say, 'Where do you think you're going?'

'Oh,' said Michael, 'we couldn't sleep. And we thought we'd go on a little explore.'

Alexandra laughed, and said to Jonathan, 'Well, we can't be cross with them, they're only doing the same thing as us.'

'Yes, but we're adults. Children shouldn't be wandering around in the middle of the night. How do you know if it's safe?'

'We weren't planning on going far,' Michael said quickly. 'Did you find anything interesting out there?'

Eleanor felt shyly impressed at the way Michael was talking to her father. He had adopted a tone she had never heard him use before, implying they were all adults together here, challenging the way Jonathan had called them children. She could see her father responding to this tactic, and filed it away as useful knowledge for the future.

Jonathan stared into the darkness and said in a contemplative tone, 'This place is structured very differently to the Clearheart Castle. Their community is much further away from the castle grounds.'

'Possibly because of the experiments,' suggested Eleanor.

'Yes,' said Michael, 'or because they're scared. Remember how Stewart said they believed the castle was haunted?'

Jonathan nodded. 'I can understand that. We used not to have much business with the castle, did we, Eleanor? It wasn't that we were afraid of it as such . . . we were just ordinary people trying to get on with our lives.' His voice tailed off. Eleanor could tell that her father's words were making Alexandra feel awkward. The four of them looked at where Jonathan and Alexandra had come from. Far in the distance there were large flaming torches and a few shack-like constructions illuminated by the flames that formed the beginning of the community. A dog started barking and Eleanor felt pleased that their explorations had come to a premature end. Jonathan said, 'Anyway, there's nothing out there you need to see. Let's go back.'

Eleanor and Michael knew better than to argue. They turned round and the group split into two. Eleanor walked back to the great hall with Alexandra. She put her arm around Eleanor's shoulders and said, 'He's funny, your father, isn't he?'

'Strange, you mean?' Eleanor asked defensively.

'No, not strange. I mean funny as in humorous. He makes me laugh. But only when we're alone together. He's so dour when we're in a group.'

'He's shy. He's not used to the sort of life you lead.'

Eleanor watched Alexandra, waiting to see how she would respond.

'Well, we all lead that life now, Eleanor,' said Alexandra, slightly sharply. 'Anyway, good night.'

'Goodnight,' said Eleanor, and returned to her room.

Chapter Seventeen

Eleanor found her dreams that night more confusing than usual. At first she dreamt about her mother, who, for some unknown reason appeared to have become good friends with Sarah. The two women were both extremely old in Eleanor's dream and sat together in a room that looked like a more elaborate version of the Kingmaker's Castle's great hall. They were drinking tea and talking about the past. Eleanor knew it was important to concentrate on what they were saying, but the harder she strained to hear the words, the fainter they became. The few fragments she did manage to make out made sense but were maddeningly elusive: 'great friends', 'different backgrounds', 'betrayal', 'honour', 'trust', 'changes over the years' and 'wanting to help'.

Before Eleanor could get to grips with what was happening, the vision changed and she had a repeat of the same dream she'd had when they were travelling. It was less of a dream than a sensation. Someone was in danger, but she had no idea who it was. When the next person she pictured in her nocturnal imaginings was Mary, she thought it must be her, but soon after she saw her friend's face, the dream sensation changed from fear to an overwhelming feeling of power and confidence. Mary was surrounded by a blazing red aura, and Eleanor felt uncertain whether it was safe to approach her friend. Then, for what felt like ages, she had an amusing, comical, but ultimately meaningless shaggy-dog story dream about Zoran and Robert trying to sell their horses to an innkeeper in exchange for a barrel of beer.

When Eleanor awoke, she had no awareness of what time it was. Checking a clock, she discovered it was much earlier than she usually arose. Just 5 a.m. But she was so awake and alert that she knew it would be impossible to get back to sleep. The others would no doubt still be in bed and Eleanor wondered what to do. She remembered the huge bathtub in the green room's *en suite* bathroom and decided to see if they had supplied her with bubble bath.

They had. Eleanor had a long soak, getting rid of some of the stiffness she always felt in her muscles when they arrived somewhere after a concentrated period of riding. Then, at about seven, she started to feel really hungry and went out into the hall. To Eleanor's surprise, James was already awake, sitting at the end of a long table eating a bowl of cornflakes, and pushing his glasses back up his long nose as he read from his huge, leather-bound book.

'Good morning, James,' she said to him.

He looked at her, startled. She gave him a little wave. He said, in a complimentary tone, 'Hello, Eleanor, I didn't realise you were a fellow lark.'

'Lark?' asked Eleanor.

'Early riser,' he explained. 'Both Stewart and I like getting up early in the morning. We consider it the best time for reading, thinking and civilised conversation. But the women . . .' He gave a heavy sigh. 'The women are night-owls. Sometimes Sophie stays in bed until midday. She says it's the sign of a true philosopher. But she's not a philosopher. Hedley's got a far greater claim to that title. At least the books she reads are by genuine thinkers instead of all that System gobbledegook.'

Eleanor swallowed. 'But she doesn't take it seriously, does she?'

'She *says* she doesn't take it seriously, but . . .' James looked at Eleanor with fresh interest, as if pleased to find someone to converse with. 'Well, it's like this. Sit down, Eleanor . . .'

She did so.

'What I think is, if you're going to study something, it might as well be something elevating. Something it's genuinely worth knowing about. I understand the logic of wanting to learn about the past by understanding what they believed, but I'm not a historian, I'm a philosopher, and I prefer to spend my time with the great minds.'

'What about your work on magic squares?'

He smiled. 'Eleanor, can I tell you a secret? All that stuff's a smokescreen. Do you know what a smoke-screen is?'

Eleanor shook her head.

'Well, the dictionaries we have date the word from a couple of thousand years ago, claiming it was, by that time, an accepted naval term. The navy, Eleanor, was an army that used to fight in boats on the sea . . .'

'Do you know a lot about army stuff?' Eleanor asked shyly.

'I know my military history, yes. Why do you ask?'

'The way my father spoke about you . . . well, it made me think you wouldn't be interested in stuff like that. Not just you,' she said quickly, seeing James's hurt face, 'but Hedley and Sophie and Stewart too. He said you were intellectuals.'

'Yes,' said James, 'that's true, we are intellectuals. But that doesn't mean we don't know about combat. Honestly, people's prejudices . . . anyway, smokescreen. Its literal meaning is an actual cloud of smoke used to disguise military operations, but it also means a ruse or device for disguising one's activities. What this means is that I pretend I'm working on theories and attempting to make important scientific discoveries, but really I just sit up in my tower all day long reading books.' He laughed. 'Would you like some cornflakes?'

Eleanor nodded and he poured her a bowl.

'It's all Stewart's fault, and the girls. They changed him, you see. Before Sophie and Hedley came along, the two of us were in perfect synch. We spent our time reading, and thinking, and leading a life of the mind. Then the girls arrived and they were much tougher and more active, and they thought we were a bit wishy-washy, so Stewart started doing all these nonsensical, elaborate, physical experiments. Sophie and Hedley thought this was absolutely fantastic and before you knew it, they looked at me as a lazy good-for-nothing. I told them I was an Epicurean, but this meant nothing to them. That's a branch of philosophy, Eleanor, mainly to do with avoiding the over-stimulation of appetite. Anyway, the point is, I had to start doing experiments too, and I didn't fancy running around the grounds, so my theories are mainly those that can be worked out with paper and pen. Mathematical questions, mostly.'

James was grinning at her as if this was the cleverest thing in the world. Eleanor smiled back, not so much impressed with his trickery as thinking what a fantastic life it must be to spend all day reading. She knew she had a secret reason for liking James, and now she knew what it was. He was much more like her than Sophie, Hedley or Stewart, and she realised that she could learn a lot from this man.

CHAPTER EIGHTEEN

Breakfast was a long drawn-out affair, and it wasn't until almost eleven that everyone had arisen and been fed. Eleanor had expected the quartet to have a precise schedule, but everyone seemed relaxed, and all that was on the agenda for the morning was a more thorough exploration of the castle grounds. James, who seemed to have grown almost as bored as Eleanor in the four hours they had sat at the breakfast table, kicked things off by asking if the group would like to come up and see the library in his tower. Eleanor agreed this would be a pleasant thing to do and they walked over to this building.

Eleanor was first up the stairs behind James and immediately went over to peruse the walls of haphazardly stacked books.

'Can we touch them?' she asked.

'By all means,' he replied. 'As long as you're careful.'

Pleased, she ran a finger along the spines, looking for something that might be interesting. When she reached a book called *King John*, she pulled it down, thinking it might be about the time before the fall of the kingdom. Like the dictionary Anderson had given her, every page had been carefully transcribed in brown ink. Looking through the first few pages, she was astonished to find the name 'Queen Eleanor' and turned to show it to Hedley, asking, 'Was there a queen called Eleanor?'

Hedley laughed. 'Yes, I believe there was. A long, long time ago. But this isn't a history book, Eleanor. It's a play by Shakespeare.'

'A play?'

'Yes, a bit like the storytellers last night, only the people acting get to say a lot more. In this play, Queen Eleanor is one of the characters.'

'Is she nice?'

Hedley took the book from Eleanor and flipped through it. 'No, I don't think so, not as far as I remember. But you have to understand that this is a play. The characters are intended to be dramatic.'

Eleanor nodded. 'I think I understand. Can I read the play, anyway?'

'Well,' she said, 'it might be a bit difficult for you. And it's not the best Shakespeare play to start with. Why don't you try a comedy like, say,' she looked along the shelf, 'here you go, *A Midsummer Night's Dream.*'

'No,' said Eleanor, 'I want to look at this one. Just for a little bit. It doesn't matter if I don't understand it.'

'Admirable sentiments,' said James, who had been eavesdropping. 'And with all due respect, Hedley, I think *King John* is a much better play than *A Midsummer Night's Dream*. There is a lesson for all the children here. I know you probably don't have much access to literature, aside from your Bibles, but if you do ever get chance to access a library, the best advice I can give to someone seeking wisdom is to read at leisure. Find your own interests, and pursue them.'

'Books aren't everything,' muttered Zoran.

'What was that?' asked James.

Zoran looked up. 'You people think wisdom comes from reading books. And it doesn't . . . it comes from experience.'

Eleanor felt embarrassed. She was really eager for the inhabitants of the Kingmaker's Castle to like them and think they were intelligent, and she knew these sort of comments from Zoran wouldn't be welcomed.

'I take it you can read,' said Stewart, in a sarcastic tone.

'Of course I can,' snapped Zoran. 'I'm just saying there's more to life than books.'

'I love reading,' said Eleanor quickly, 'and writing stories. Although I haven't done that much recently. At first I thought I'd write a diary about my adventures, but I never know when is the best time to write things. Last thing at night I'm always too tired, and the following morning I'm too excited about the day ahead to think about what happened yesterday. I think the best thing will be to wait until I have some time back at the Clearheart Castle and then write up the experiences I had on each expedition.'

'That's a good idea, Eleanor,' said James, admiringly. 'This is an extremely interesting moment in history. An account such as the one you describe could be very useful when people look back on this period.'

'Why is this period so interesting?' asked Lucinda, brushing her hair back from her face.

'Well,' he said, 'I realise this is hard for you to understand because we live in an age when the concept of a collective record is almost impossible to imagine, but there is no way that England will stay the way it is for much longer. For the first time in thousands of years, we are living in a state of almost complete anarchy. I realise this isn't how it seems, thanks to the way each castle and community regulates itself, but what people don't realise is that the fall of the kingdom came at the end of a long period of decentralization. It is a time that has always been predicted, by poets and philosophers, and feared by politicians, a word that seems almost meaningless now, although we do still have them – people like Basker, for example. But while some saw this possible future as a utopia, and some as a dystopia, what they all failed to realise was that this period of anarchy would in itself be temporary. We have entered a new Dark Age. The period we are living in now can be seen as similar to the *Völkerwanderung* – the wandering of the peoples – out of which grew a number of successor kingdoms, each ruled over by the barbarians who inherited the ruins of the Western Empire. But we have yet to discover how order will be restored. And it is inevitable that this will happen.'

'Not inevitable, surely,' said Sarah, in a soft voice.

He turned to her. 'The only way it won't happen is if a dominant force fails to emerge. It may take years of skirmishes, but the moment someone with sufficient strength establishes themselves, we will see a return to the old order. Unless, of course, we are attacked from overseas, and even then the same thing will happen, only with a foreign power instead of a homegrown one. So, to answer your initial question, Lucinda, this period is interesting because it is a moment in a cycle that only occurs once in several millennia.'

James's speech had silenced everyone. Eleanor had struggled to understand it, and wished she had a recording of his words to analyse on her own. It was obvious to her that people weren't speaking because they knew James was right, and even if they didn't understand exactly what he had said, it was clear that it had come from years of serious study. It was Stewart who broke the tension, asking, 'Shall we go outside? I've got something fun for us all to do.'

CHAPTER
NINETEEN

'Is this an experiment?' Hephzi asked as Stewart handed her a large diamond-shaped piece of blue plastic wrapped around a wooden frame and attached to a long length of twine.

He laughed. 'No. It would be possible to use it for an experiment. Science is all around us. But, no, this is purely for your enjoyment.'

'What are these things?' asked Beth.

'Kites,' said Zoran.

Stewart looked up. 'You've played with one before?'

Zoran seemed pleased by the attention. 'Of course. We used to make them when we were children.'

'Oh,' said Stewart, 'I didn't realise people still did that. I thought it had fallen out of fashion.'

'Zoran didn't grow up with the rest of us,' Alexandra explained. 'He knows about things that we don't know about. Traditions.'

This surprised Eleanor, who had always imagined

that the Castle Six had known each other since childhood, even though they were different ages and Alexandra had previously explained this wasn't the case. She waited for Zoran or Alexandra to say something further, but they both kept quiet. Stewart continued down the line, giving Eleanor a yellow kite. Zoran was already unravelling his, and showing others how to get their kite flying. Eleanor copied them, and running along, soon managed to get her kite into the air. She stopped and Stewart came up behind her, putting his hands on her shoulders.

'That's it,' he said, 'you've got it. See how the tail flaps out behind it. Yes, that's brilliant.'

Eleanor felt pleased. She controlled the kite for a moment, and then it nose-dived and she failed to stop it plummeting to the floor. Looking round at the smiling faces of the others, she felt happy and relaxed, no longer ashamed of her comrades and pleased to be part of such a good-natured group.

Eleanor was relieved to see that lunch was a plate of fish and vegetables rather than another serving of last night's unpleasant stew. As she picked up her fork and started to tuck into it, Beth turned to her and asked, 'So, have you spoken to him?'

She didn't like to lie. 'Yes,' she said, 'we did have a conversation.'

'At breakfast?'

'No,' she replied, 'last night.'

Beth tapped her arm. 'You went to his room? I didn't want you to do that. You weren't supposed to make it look obvious.'

'Relax,' said Eleanor. 'That's not how it happened. He came to my room.'

'What?' demanded Beth. 'Why?'

'It's just something he does sometimes. He knows I have trouble getting to sleep and he likes to go on a little explore when we arrive somewhere new.'

Beth seemed irritated by this. Eleanor realised she was jealous, and felt ashamed that she was pleased to have aroused this emotion in her friend. Beth said, 'Why doesn't he go exploring with me? I don't go to sleep straight away either. Actually, as far as I know, nor does my sister.'

Eleanor remembered what Michael had said last night about how it was more fun to go exploring with her than his girlfriend. This made her feel proud, and then ashamed again. She wondered what was wrong with her that made her want to interfere with her friends' relationships in this way. Boredom? Mischievousness? Most of all, she suddenly realised, it was because she was feeling lonely. Her last adventure had been so much more enjoyable for her, meeting Justin and helping him fight against his family. If only she had managed to persuade him to leave his castle and come travelling with her.

'Well,' said Eleanor, 'I don't really know why he comes to my room, he just does. Do you want to know what he said or not?'

'Yes, of course I do. Tell me!'

'He said he enjoyed acting with you. But he mentioned Hephzi too.'

Beth scowled, clearly exasperated. 'Well, what's that supposed to mean?'

'I think he's definitely in love with your sister.'

'Oh, Eleanor, you're no use,' she sighed, turning round so her back was towards her.

'I'm sorry, Beth, that's just how it seems.'

'How it *seems*, Eleanor, that's the whole point.'

CHAPTER
TWENTY

After lunch, the group was split into four, each unit going off with a different member of the Kingmaker's Quartet. Eleanor, Alexandra, Beth and Sarah went with Sophie to her tower. She made them all tea, and they sat with her around a circular wooden table.

'Oh,' she said, 'we're going to enjoy ourselves this afternoon. You mustn't tell the others about what we're going to do now, OK? They all think this sort of thing is really stupid. And I suppose it is, really, but it's also lots of fun.'

'What are we going to do?'

Sophie stood up. 'Come and help me, Eleanor.'

The two of them went through into another small room and came back carrying a large white board. Sophie put the board up against a wall and placed a chair in front of it.

'OK,' she said, 'let's start with you, Sarah. Can you sit in the chair, please?'

She did so. Sophie stood in front of it. She looked at Sarah, walked back, squinted, and looked again. 'Oh,' she said, 'it doesn't seem to be working today. Unless . . . oh yes, that could be it . . . Sarah, could you put your arm just above your head? Yes, that's right, like that. Gosh . . . I don't see that often. But it's clear. My goodness, it's clear. Your aura's white.'

'My what?' Sarah asked.

'Your aura. It's like a sphere of coloured light that emanates from your physical form. I put the white board behind you to make it easier to see as most people have coloured auras. But yours is almost dazzlingly white. Wow.'

'What does that mean?'

'Well, purity. It's the colour of spiritual energy. Are you religious, Sarah?'

'I'm a Christian.'

'I see. There's nothing wrong with you. It's clear you have great power, and dedicated belief. You're strong, Sarah, as strong as they come.'

Sarah gave a small smile. 'Thank you.'

She stood up.

'Who's next?' asked Sophie.

'Me,' said Beth, eagerly jumping into the chair. 'Shall I put my arm behind my head too?'

'No, no, that's not necessary. Your aura is obvious. I can almost see it without the white behind you.'

'What colour is it?'

'Red.'

'What does that mean?'

'Are you angry, Beth?'

'Angry?'

'Yes, is there something . . . or someone . . . annoying you at the moment?'

Eleanor couldn't stop herself laughing. Beth turned and gave her a cross look, then said, 'Yes. You. My aura's not red. Have another look.'

Sophie smiled. 'I'm sorry, Beth, it's definitely red. What you need to do is calm down the vibration by swapping bedrooms with Eleanor and spending the night in the green room.'

'Whatever,' said Beth, scowling and jumping off the chair. Alexandra took her place.

'Ah,' said Sophie, 'this is interesting, you have two colours in your aura. One is slight, but it's definitely there. In fact, I think that's your normal aura and the other colour has come in on top of it. Like Beth, I think you are in a period of possible emotional conflict or change. Normally, it looks like your aura is mainly blue, which is a healing colour. Do you sleep well, Alexandra?'

'Yes,' she said, 'usually very well.'

'And what about your dreams? Do you remember them?'

'Sometimes. Not always.'

'Hmm. If you're interested, with some work, it might be possible for you to experience lucid dreaming.'

Alexandra shook her head. 'That's not my sort of thing. What other colour do you see?'

'Orange. It means that at the moment your emotions are in slight disarray and you need to focus on finding harmony again. This is only a temporary problem, nothing to worry about, but it's probably best to act now rather than letting the orange emotion overwhelm your healing powers.'

Alexandra nodded. 'You may have a point. I think I understand what you're referring to.'

'That's good. Not everyone has such emotional awareness. Eleanor, would you like to sit in the chair?'

She did so. Sophie nodded. 'Yes, I thought so. Your aura is immediately apparent. It's very strong too. You have a green aura. Green is associated with the heart, and this tells me that it is time you faced up to your true emotions. You've been hiding from yourself, Eleanor.'

Eleanor had no problem swapping bedrooms with Beth when the time came. She wouldn't have wanted to sleep on the floor of the spy tower like Hephzibah, but Beth's tower, if not as luxurious as the green bedroom, was a pleasant place to spend the night. She half-expected Michael or Beth to come and visit her again, but if anyone else was still awake they didn't bother

her. Disappointed not to be disturbed, Eleanor dragged a chair across to the window and sat staring out over the grounds of the Kingmaker's Castle. Her head was full of thoughts of the day, especially James's speech on the state of England, which she'd hoped to decipher when she had time on her own, but which she now struggled to reassemble. It frustrated her that by the time she did finally get to write down her experiences, the details would no doubt have almost entirely gone. It was the same with the conversation she'd had with Justin at the Greengrove Castle about other kingdoms beyond this one. She rubbed a knuckle against her forehead, urging herself to remember what James had said. There was a desk on the other side of the tower. She went over to it, opened the left drawer and found a red pencil along with a small pad. Eleanor knew it would be hard to hang on to a sheet of paper during her travels and was only writing this down in the hope that inscribing the words would burn the information into her memory. Aware that she would be unable to carry more than a few details in her head, she tried to compress what she did remember into a few essential sentences:

1 We are living in a new Dark Age.
2 The world was not always like this.
3 The world will not always be like this.
4 One day, order will be restored.

This last sentence made Eleanor feel sad and happy at the same time. Sad because it had never occurred to her that the period she lived in was a dark age; happy because she believed she would see the day when all the communities within her country would be reunited again. Once again she thought about how she had both lost and gained so much since she travelled beyond the grounds of her own castle. The main thing she had lost was innocence; it was impossible for her to return to the blissful, but boring, state of ignorance she'd lived in for most of her life. Finding out that her country could be so much more meant that she would be dissatisfied until this state of perfection was achieved, but it also meant that her struggle was worth something, and any hardship she suffered while in the service of the Castle Six could be understood as contributing to the greater good. It was reassuring to discover that she was not just helping the people of the Clearheart Community, but also everyone in England.

And if she died in the process, her death would be a noble one.

CHAPTER TWENTY-ONE

At first Eleanor assumed she was still in the middle of a nightmare. Then she realised someone really was shaking her as hard as they could and opened her eyes. It was her father, Jonathan, and he looked frightened.

'Wake up, Ellie, get dressed.'

'Why? What's happening?'

'There's no time to explain. Please, you have to get ready, as quick as you can.'

Jonathan had turned round and was already hurrying down the tower's spiral steps. Eleanor jumped out of bed, changed out of her nightie into her blue dress, and grabbed her large leather bag. Shoving her nightie inside, she ran after her father.

'Is it the people here? Are they evil?'

'No,' said Jonathan. 'It's Mary – she's been kidnapped.'

'What?' asked Eleanor.

The rest of the Castle Six and all the other children

were waiting outside, already mounted. Jonathan jumped up onto his horse, and then reached out his arm to help Eleanor. The group immediately started to ride at serious speed, picking out a route through the darkness. It was just before dawn, and Eleanor felt tired, although fear for her friend had sent adrenalin coursing round her system. No one seemed to want to talk and it ,was fifteen minutes before they started to slow slightly and she could ask Alexandra, 'Where are we going?'

'Back to the Clearheart Castle.'

'How long ago was Mary kidnapped?'

'Two days. It's taken that long for the messenger to reach us.'

'Then why are we going back to our castle? She won't be there now.'

'They think she might've been taken into the wilderness.'

'Who does?'

'Mary's parents. The people at our castle. Does it matter? Why are you asking so many questions?'

Eleanor dropped back away from Alexandra. Then she turned her horse round and rode off in the opposite direction.

'Wait,' shouted Alexandra after her. 'Where are you going?'

Chapter Twenty-Two

'Eleanor!' exclaimed James. 'What are you doing back here?'

'I need to talk to you. All of you.'

James rubbed his hands against his trousers. 'Of course. But what's wrong?'

Eleanor didn't answer, instead jumping down from her horse.

'OK,' he said, 'tie up your horse and go to the great hall. I'll get the others.'

Eleanor did as she was told. When she reached the great hall she sat on the left-hand side of the large table and waited. The Kingmaker's Quartet entered together, taking seats opposite her. Sophie looked more tired than the others and kept blinking. James was the first to speak. 'What is it, Eleanor?'

'I need your advice.'

'OK,' he replied, calmly. 'Is this about the girl who's

vanished from your community?'

'Yes,' said Eleanor. 'I know who kidnapped her. And it's all my fault.'

'Are you serious?' asked Sophie.

'Yes.'

'OK, Eleanor,' asked James, 'who was it?'

'Anderson.'

'Anderson?' Sophie exclaimed. 'How can you know this? And how is it your fault?'

Eleanor sighed. 'I knew this would come back to haunt me. I've had nightmares about it, and felt a terrible sense of guilt ever since I made this mistake. When we went to the Greengrove Castle, I . . . well, I told Anderson that Mary admired him. At the time he said he wasn't interested in hearing about that sort of thing, but he must've been lying, and gone back to get her.'

James and Sophie exchanged a look.

'What?' demanded Eleanor. 'What is it? Tell me.'

'Well,' said James, after a pause, 'news reached us recently . . . from one of our spies . . .'

'They're not spies,' said Hedley, angrily.

'OK, not spies, just people who . . . gather information for us. They found out that Anderson and Katharine have taken over the Kinder Castle.'

'Where you used to live?' asked Eleanor.

'Exactly. They're trying to turn the children into an army, and they're planning to attack the Baldwin Castle.'

Eleanor was flabbergasted that the Kingmaker's Quartet could sit there and calmly reveal they had this information. She wondered if she had misjudged them, and felt so angry about their calmness that she struggled to keep her voice down even as she asked them, 'You knew about this? And you didn't try to stop it?'

'Eleanor, we're not that sort of castle,' said Sophie, in a conciliatory voice, 'or community. We don't have an army, we don't need one as we don't really have any fear of invasion, because it's not just the community that believe the horror stories about the ghosts and plagues that they believe are in our castle.'

'Couldn't you have told someone else?' Eleanor demanded, exasperated. 'Some kind of peace-keeping force?'

'We've warned the Baldwin Castle. They're doing everything they can to prepare themselves.'

Eleanor shook her head. 'But . . . if you'd told us sooner, if we'd had time to prepare . . . what can we do now?'

'This is a time for action, Eleanor,' said James, not responding to her anger. 'You must go back to the Castle Six, tell them not to return to your castle, but to go straight to the Baldwin Castle. It's unlikely you'll get there before the invasion starts, but the connection you and your group has with Katharine, Anderson and Mary may help you resolve this situation. You may well encounter violence, but you have been trained to deal with this, Eleanor The children of the Kinder Castle will be an undisciplined, unruly army. Be careful, think clearly, and remember, whatever happens, we're proud of you.'

Eleanor stood up, and left the room. James's words hadn't completely calmed her, but she saw the logic in what he'd said, and realised that the Kingmaker's Quartet could be of no further assistance. It was up to her now.

CHAPTER TWENTY-THREE

They had started early, two hours before sunrise. Anderson kept telling the group that this would be an easy battle, but he still wanted to do everything he could to make sure it went smoothly, starting off by ensuring they had the element of surprise. Mary sensed that in spite of his outward show of confidence, Anderson was more anxious than he let on. Last night she had overheard him talking to Katharine and he'd said something about how this would be a 'symbolic victory'. She hadn't understood what he'd meant at the time, but thinking about it further she realised it was tied in with the talk they'd had when Anderson first took her from her parents. Looking round at the army of unruly children behind her, it was hard to square Anderson's noble notions with the physical reality of what was about to happen, but there was definitely something exciting about the way he thought. At first Mary had been terrified of him, then too flattered by his attentions to take what he was saying seriously; now she wondered whether there might be some truth to his argument that they were alike.

She definitely felt different from her parents. Eleanor's father had joined the Castle Six, but Mary couldn't imagine her parents approving of attacking another community. She was surprised to find herself looking forward to fighting. She had her crossbow, and bag of rocks, and felt excited about the battle. There was something about being part of a group that felt different from anything she'd experienced before. Even when she had spent her afternoons with the gang of teenagers by the river, she had rarely spoken to anyone, and really it had been like going there alone. Eleanor was her only real friend, and it was only now that she realised how lonely she'd felt when Eleanor started having adventures without her. When that happened, Mary's attitude to life had changed dramatically. Before then, Mary had paid little attention to life inside the Castle. She'd noticed Anderson occasionally, in church or walking around their community, but that was all. She saw no reason why her life should be any different from her parents', and although she often got in trouble with her teachers, she'd tried her best to excel in school. The reason why Mary got in trouble was that she hated bullying, and whenever she witnessed it she felt compelled to step in. Her teachers tended to turn a blind eye to this sort of thing, seeing it as all part of the rough-and-tumble of childhood, and seemed angrier with her for bringing it to their attention than they were with the culprits. But she'd always performed well in class, and enjoyed a friendly competitiveness with Eleanor. Now, though, she could no longer see the point of studying hard. Her lessons had little to do with life outside school, and Anderson seemed to think her education had such little value that she should be happy to surrender it. And that was assuming they returned to their community and she didn't live out the rest of her days in the wilderness and other people's castles.

Mary turned round. Katharine had ridden up alongside her. She worried Katharine was going to tell her off, but instead she said, 'Mary, can I talk to you for a minute?'

'Of course. What's wrong?'

'I want to apologise for the way I've treated you. When I think I almost pushed your face into a plate of food, well, I can scarcely believe it.'

'It's OK.'

Katharine shook her head. 'No, it's not OK. I don't know what's been wrong with me. I've been under a lot of stress, and to be perfectly honest, I couldn't understand why Anderson thought it was so important to go back and collect you from your community. But now I realise what he sees in you. I envy you, Mary, getting to the right path so young. It's taken me years to learn what you already know now.

'I don't know how much you know about my past, but I assume your friend Eleanor has probably spoken to you about me?'

Katharine swivelled on her saddle so she could make eye contact with Mary, who was riding slightly behind her. Mary didn't know what to say. She assumed that Anderson had told Katharine she thought they were evil when he first abducted her, although given the taciturn mood he'd been in over the last few days, this wasn't certain, but as far as she could remember she hadn't said anything specific to him about Katharine.

'A bit, yes . . .'

Katharine nodded. 'I do feel guilty about what happened at the Greengrove Castle. But we were there the whole time, and did our best to make sure no one got too upset. We were imprisoned along with Eleanor, and we managed to avoid having a sword fight. It's hard being an undercover agent. Look, I don't expect Eleanor to understand, and I don't care if she never forgives me. But I would like to have a proper friendship with you. We got off to a bad start, but there's no reason why that should influence the whole of our relationship.'

Mary hadn't expected this. She had assumed Katharine would always be her enemy, the pain she would have to suffer as a price for the pleasure of her friendship with Anderson. Katharine's whole demeanour was much softer than usual today, which seemed odd given that they were riding into battle. Still feeling slightly suspicious, she said, as a test, 'I understand why you don't like me . . .'

'Mary,' said Katharine sharply, 'I've never not liked you. I know I get angry with you, but the truth is, there are so many children at the Kingmaker's Castle, and so many of them are so badly behaved, that I've stopped seeing them as human beings. I know you're not really a child . . . not in the way Andrew and Simon are children . . . but in that moment, when I snapped with you, I didn't really see you as you, as a person, more as an animal who wasn't doing what it was supposed to be doing.'

Mary continued riding alongside Katharine, fascinated by this insight into her thought processes. She seemed so much less diplomatic than Anderson, even incapable of apologising for an insult without making things worse. So she had thought of her as an animal? How was she supposed to respond to that? And yet Katharine spoke these words as if she was explaining herself to another adult, and believed there was no way Mary could fail to understand. Mary thought for a moment, and then decided it would be much safer to have Katharine as a friend than an enemy, and thought that Anderson would probably be pleased rather than angry to see the two of them getting along. In a careful voice, Mary replied, 'I would be proud to be your friend, Katharine.'

Katharine smiled, reached out to ruffle Mary's hair, and then rode ahead.

CHAPTER TWENTY-FOUR

It took Eleanor longer to locate the Castle Six than she'd anticipated. At first the tracks had been so easy to follow that she'd assumed she'd find her friends in no time at all. But as she kept going, she found spots where their paths were hard to make out and even a couple of places near spots of wilderness where they had ridden through earth that had recently been disturbed by previous travellers. So she was relieved when she saw Hephzi in the distance, riding her white horse at the back of the group. 'Hephzi!' she shouted.

Hephzi turned and smiled. 'Eleanor!' Then she said to the others. 'Look, everyone. Ellie's back.'

Jonathan rode back to her and shouted, 'Where have you been, Eleanor? You had us alarmed and now really isn't a very good time to throw a strop. Mary could be in terrible danger.'

'I wasn't throwing a strop. I was finding out where Mary is being kept.'

'What? How did you do that?'

'Dad, listen to me. I know who's kidnapped Mary.'

'Who?'

'Anderson.'

Jonathan went silent and pursed his lips. Eleanor knew what her father was thinking. He had never forgiven Anderson for endangering Eleanor's life when she had gone on her previous mission. She also knew that he had always regretted not fighting him the last time the two men faced each other. The fact that he had kidnapped Mary clearly outraged Jonathan, but at the same time Eleanor could tell her father would relish the opportunity to face Anderson again.

'Where has he taken her?' he asked.

'He took her to the Kinder Castle.'

'Right. Let's go there.'

Eleanor shook her head. 'No. They've already moved on. They're heading to attack the Baldwin Castle.'

'The Baldwin Castle? Where's that?'

'James made me a map. It's not too far from here. We probably won't be able to get there in time to stop the battle, but we can definitely help them win it.'

'OK, Eleanor. Alexandra, look at this map and work out the best route.'

CHAPTER TWENTY-FIVE

Anderson rode up alongside Mary and put his hand on her shoulder. Up ahead, she could see the overweight brothers, Andrew and Stephen, leading the army. With their spiky blond hair and matching orange-and-yellow-striped suits, they were an unusual sight, vibrant even in the early morning light.

The other children trailed for an incredible distance behind them, snaking out far across the countryside. Mary turned slightly and led her horse alongside Anderson's.

'Katharine said she had a good conversation with you.'

Mary nodded.

'I'm pleased,' he said, 'I want you two to be friends.' He spat on the ground. 'How are you feeling, Mary?'

'OK. Why?'

'Are you scared? Excited? Looking forward to fighting?'

'Yes,' she said. 'I mean, to the last one.'

He smiled. 'We're very close, you realise. The Baldwin Castle is only about five minutes away.'

Mary nodded. Her stomach felt tense and she knew she wouldn't relax until the fight had started. Anderson turned away from her and rode back down the line of the army, making sure everyone had their catapults or crossbows up and were ready to fight.

The original plan had been to surround the front entrance of the Baldwin Castle, attack the community until the army rose up and then drive back both army and community until they could invade the castle. But as soon as they came in sight of the castle, it was obvious that the Baldwin Castle army had been forewarned and were waiting for them.

Within seconds, Mary found herself caught up in a battle. Baldwin Castle's army was much smaller in number than the children's, but as fully trained adults, its soldiers were much more adept at fighting. Armed mainly with staffs, they were attempting to knock the mounted children from their rides and shove back those who were running towards them.

The catapults and crossbows worked best from a distance, and the children's army split into two flanks: the right side retreating up the hill to get a better vantage point, the left engaging in hand-to-hand combat. The bigger, tougher children pulled the staffs from their opponents and used them against them, hundreds of bodies combining in a busy scrum.

Dust was rising up from the ground and Mary found it hard to see. She kept reloading her crossbow and firing blindly, uncertain whether any of her stones were reaching their targets. It was obvious that she couldn't move forward, but she worried that to retreat with the others would seem like cowardice. More than anything, Mary wanted Anderson to be proud of her. She looked around desperately, wondering where he was, but the dust was so thick and the action so fast that she couldn't see him. Suddenly, Mary felt an arm swoop round her waist. Somebody had grabbed hold of her and was trying to get her up onto their horse. She couldn't see who it was and was terrified that it might be someone from the rival army. She wriggled and kicked, but couldn't get free. Then, when she was up on the back of the horse, she saw it was Katharine.

'Mary,' Katherine said, 'I think it would be better if you come up higher with me. This battle's going to take much longer than we anticipated.'

CHAPTER TWENTY-SIX

Eleanor was starving. She knew she couldn't ask if they could stop somewhere to eat, but wished they'd had breakfast before leaving the Kingmaker's Castle. The morning's exertion had left her exhausted and her stomach was so empty she could feel it grumbling. When she saw an inn in the distance, one of these strange, makeshift buildings that she had noticed once or twice on her travels, different from the stone inns closer to communities, usually near a more populated patch of wilderness, she was so surprised that at first she thought it was a mirage.

'Jonathan,' shouted Alexandra, 'maybe we should run in here. Just for some bread and water.'

Jonathan looked at the inn. 'I'm not sure. It doesn't look like the sort of place that would welcome travellers.'

'I'm not saying we should all go in. Just one of us. You, Jonathan, or maybe Zoran.'

'I'll go,' said Zoran. 'I'm not scared of these places.'

The group stopped. Zoran climbed down from his horse and went over to the inn. There was a man standing outside the corrugated-iron shack. He was wearing a stained brown leather apron and had a large white whiskery moustache that took up most of the bottom half of his face. Eleanor could tell everyone was tense, waiting to see what would happen when Zoran went over to him. But it seemed fine. The man stepped back without comment and allowed Zoran inside.

Moments later, Zoran emerged with an orange string bag of bread rolls and a huge barrel of water. Eleanor ran over to him and asked, 'Please can I have a roll, Zoran? I'm so hungry.'

'Sure,' he replied, handing her one. 'Give me your water-bottle and I'll fill that up too.'

Eleanor did so, then tried to eat her bread roll. Her mouth was dry and the bread was hard to swallow. Zoran handed her water-bottle back and she used it to dampen the bread. Then she got back onto her horse Nathaniel.

As they continued their journey to the Baldwin Castle, Eleanor was troubled by guilty thoughts. It irritated her that doing something so small – telling Anderson that Mary had a crush on him during their previous mission – had created so much trouble. It was obvious that this was the reason he had kidnapped her friend, and the only thing that gave her hope was that Anderson had so few supporters that he was unlikely to do anything to alienate or hurt Mary. Eleanor thought she had already amply paid for this sin when first Anderson then Mary had been cross with her, but it seemed that she would continue to be haunted by this trivial crime. She knew she was in the wrong, but still kept trying to lessen what she had done in her mind. She told herself that when she'd confided in Anderson she had no idea he was a bad person and just wanted a firmer friendship with him. Was that so wrong? And he had lied too, telling her he had no interest in this information when it was clearly important to him. But no matter how she tried to rationalise it, she still felt bad. Frustrated, Eleanor shook her head, trying to get these thoughts out of her mind, and rode faster.

Chapter
Twenty-Seven

Katharine set Mary down on the side of the hill, and jumped down beside her. She rolled over in the long grass and lay flat, holding out her crossbow, targeting someone from the opposing army and firing a stone.

'Go on,' she told Mary, 'get your crossbow out.'

She did so, then put her bag of stones in the grass alongside her, and loaded the crossbow. As she was about to fire, Katharine turned to her and snapped, 'What are you doing? That's no good. Aim for their heads. Aim for their *eyes*.'

Mary was shocked. 'But Anderson said we shouldn't try to hurt the soldiers, just drive them back.'

Katharine snorted. 'A stone fired from a crossbow is going to hurt no matter where you hit someone. You might as well take them down.' She laughed and fired another stone. Mary didn't know what to do, so she raised the crossbow to the height Katharine instructed, but deliberately moved the bow so the stone would miss her target. Katharine didn't seem to notice, too engrossed in firing her own stones. She saw a splatter of blood splash out from a soldier's ear.

'You know, thousands of years ago, they used to believe that crossbows were the instrument of the devil,' said Katharine, loading another stone, 'but that was just envy. Anyone who actually had a crossbow realised they were a wonderful creation. The precision, the force, the sheer pleasure of firing one of these things. And, yes, hitting your target.'

Mary didn't like this kind of talk. It sounded so malevolent, so different from Anderson's high ideas. He didn't seem to like the idea of fighting, or causing pain, and merely saw it as a necessary evil. Katharine seemed to relish hurting people.

'Oh, I know some people see these kind of weapons as much more informal than hand-to-hand combat,' she continued, 'but again, those are individuals who never rise above the lure of brute force. They don't understand the intellectual elegance of considered violence.'

Mary shuddered.

'Does the way I talk disturb you?' Katharine asked. 'It shouldn't. I realise you're young, Mary, and this is a lot to take in. But it's important not to be afraid of your natural instincts. I'm not saying you should go in search of conflict, but when it arises, there's no harm in enjoying it.' She fired a stone. 'This is the path you've chosen.'

Mary caught sight of Anderson among the crowd. He was pulling a staff away from one of the rival army. When he had successfully taken it from him he turned and, with a fast upswing, caught his opponent hard beneath the chin. The man fell backwards, but instead of taking advantage of this, Anderson ran back to his horse and rode up to where Mary and Katharine were positioned on the hill. He then jumped down, lifted Katharine in his arms and kissed her on the lips.

'What do you think?' Katharine asked, as they broke apart.

'It's hard. It's going to take much longer than we expected. But what I don't understand is, who told them we were coming?'

'Spies?' suggested Katharine.

'At the Kinder Castle?' he asked. 'Who would be recruiting children? And why would they want to warn the Baldwin Castle? It doesn't make sense.'

'Maybe the spies aren't actually inside the castle. Someone could've been watching us. Tracking our movements.'

'Oh, Katharine, now you're being paranoid. But I will admit there is something strange going on.'

Anderson turned away from them, looking down over the battlefield. The children who had retreated to the hill were now forced to come forward, as those in the front line were being knocked down and left, concussed, on the grass. He shook his head, and then took Katharine and Mary's hands.

'Come on,' he said, 'they need us down there.'

CHAPTER TWENTY-EIGHT

They could see the fighting from a distance. Jonathan stopped and got everyone to form a circle.

'OK,' he said, 'there's no point in us taking on the whole army. But, remember, these are children, and our best chance of winning this fight is to intimidate them.'

'How are we going to do that?'

'By capturing Anderson and Katharine. If we focus our attention on doing that, then the children will get scared and they will be easy to control.'

'But what happens if we get caught up in the fighting?' asked Stefan. 'Should we use our swords?'

Jonathan shook his head. 'No. This isn't that kind of battle. It looks like they're fighting with sticks and stones, and we don't want any casualties. But if you do get trapped, don't be afraid to use your fists.'

Eleanor looked round at the group. She could tell everyone was more scared by the prospect of fighting with their fists than they were of using swords. Their initial training at the Clearheart Castle had involved several days of mock battles with wooden replica swords, and although they'd yet to have a real opportunity to put these skills into action, the muscles and knowledge were there, whereas unarmed combat remained a scary prospect.

Jonathan split the group into two. Eleanor was placed with her father, Sarah, Alexandra, and the twins. There was no question which of the couple they were going for.

'He's mine,' said Jonathan, turning and screaming a war-cry as he led the charge into the scrum of bodies twisting and fighting below.

CHAPTER
TWENTY-NINE

Mary felt exhilarated as she charged into battle with Anderson and Katharine. Within seconds, the two adults had separated, and Mary had to choose which one to remain alongside. She went after Anderson, feeling safer with him. Anderson noticed her presence and seemed pleased, telling her to grab one soldier's staff as he punched him in the face. Once she had this weapon she felt safer, moving back and, encouraged by Anderson, swinging it at another soldier. It connected, and the soldier fell backwards, visibly injured. But this didn't disturb Mary in the same way Katharine's encouragement had. The battle didn't seem so uneven, and it was easy for her to justify her action as self-defence.

The fighting children and soldiers were packed so tightly together that after this blow it was momentarily impossible for Anderson and Mary to do anything more elaborate than attempt to stay upright. Several soldiers unexpectedly fell backwards and Anderson and Mary were swept into a sudden eddy of people and separated again. The crowd pushed forward and Mary felt a crush of pain in her chest as the wind was knocked out of her. She stared straight ahead, trying not to panic. She could see Andrew and Stephen at the front of the pack, only a few rows of soldiers left between them and the drawbridge, which was down, leading to where the portcullis remained up. Mary couldn't understand why the Baldwin Castle army hadn't taken the basic steps of pulling up the drawbridge and bringing down the portcullis to protect the building from invasion should the children be successful in this battle, and she worried that there might be another trap waiting for them within the castle grounds. She wanted to voice this concern to Anderson but he was far away from her now, having manoeuvred himself into a position where he could fight again.

Summoning up all her strength, Mary shoved the backs of the people in front of her, and pulled up her staff, ready to strike another blow. But before she could do so, she heard a familiar voice shouting her name.

CHAPTER THIRTY

Eleanor was astonished to see Mary, staff aloft, about to hit a soldier. Any concern she had for her friend disappeared and she felt a sudden fury, shouting Mary's name at the top of her voice.

Mary turned round. As she did so, the soldier facing her grabbed her staff. Mary whirled back round, shoving the soldier as hard as she could. Eleanor pushed her way through the children in front of her and tried to grab hold of Mary. The two of them tussled, but Eleanor managed to get her arms around her waist and started pulling her backwards, ignoring Mary's struggles and trying not to fall backwards. The crowd seemed startled by two people trying to get away from the castle rather than heading towards it, and moved aside, allowing the pair of them through.

'Hold still,' Eleanor told the flailing Mary, stopping to pull a thick strand of the girl's red hair out of her mouth.

'Let go,' shouted Mary. 'You're hurting me.'

They started to back up the hill, when Mary got the better of Eleanor, and broke away. She ran a few steps before Eleanor dived at her legs and brought her down. The two of them rolled in the grass, before separating, both out of breath. They were a safe distance from the action now, and Eleanor lay there waiting for Mary to try something. Instead she said, 'I don't know why you're angry with me. This is all your fault.'

'My fault?' Eleanor demanded.

'You told Anderson . . .'

'I know,' said Eleanor, 'and I realise that was wrong. But I don't see how that leads to you fighting in a battle. Unless you're claiming that Anderson brainwashed you?'

Mary laughed. 'He hasn't brainwashed me. And he's not evil. At least no more than you.'

Eleanor was astonished. 'You think I'm evil?'

'No,' she said, 'but I don't think Anderson is either. He explained what happened at the Greengrove Castle.'

'Yeah?' asked Eleanor. 'If he's so good, why did he run away from us and why has he got you involved in this battle?'

Mary didn't speak for a moment, and Eleanor could tell she was still trying to get her breath back. 'He cares about me. He thinks I'm important. He said that one day he thinks I'm going to be the Queen of England.'

Eleanor stared at her friend. It hadn't occurred to

her that Anderson would have done such a good job of manipulating her. She supposed it wasn't that surprising: Anderson was charming, and if he gave Mary his undivided attention it was easy to see why she would be flattered.

'Mary,' she said gently, 'no one doubts that you're a special person.'

'Yeah, right,' answered Mary. 'Just not as special as you.'

'Why are you saying this? I thought we were friends.'

'We were. Until you went away. You completely abandoned me, Ellie, and expected me to feel excited about what was happening for you. But what about me? What about my life?'

Mary's anguished cry hurt Eleanor, and she felt a sudden rush of conflicting emotions. More than anything she wanted Mary to stop acting like this, to go back to being the happy good-natured companion she'd known in the Clearheart Community, and she thought that if she could just give her a hug maybe it would remind her of all the times they'd shared together. But the person standing in front of her looked like she would respond to any physical affection with a punch.

'You're still my closest friend, Mary,' Eleanor began tentatively. 'I don't feel the same way about Hephzi or Beth that I do about you.'

Mary rolled her eyes.

'OK,' said Eleanor, changing tack. 'I accept what you're saying. I did get overexcited when I was chosen by the Castle Seven . . .'

'Just a little bit,' Mary mocked.

Eleanor pressed on. 'But then when I came back from my mission and everything had gone wrong, I thought you understood that my friendship with you was more important than anything. As long as I've known you, Mary, you've always been a good person, and hated any form of bullying. And now I find you here, doing the one thing you've always despised.'

'What?' laughed Mary. 'You think this is bullying? This is a battle. It's noble and important and the first step to restoring things to the way they were.'

'What's so great about the way things were, Mary?'

Mary looked surprised. 'Isn't that what everyone wants? To be the one person who's in charge?'

Eleanor sighed. 'I don't know. Maybe that's what Anderson wants. Maybe that's what Katharine wants. Maybe it's even what you want. I can understand why you feel proud that they said that you could be Queen. But the Castle Six is different from the Castle Seven. Now my father's in charge everyone is honest with each other.'

She turned, took a deep breath, and made a direct appeal to her friend. 'You should've seen the people I met at the castle we just went to, Mary. They were different from us. They called themselves intellectuals and it was obvious that they had huge brains, but they also had big hearts. They understood that there's more to England's future than constant fighting.'

Mary pointed down at the battlefield. 'Well, your father clearly wasn't paying attention.'

CHAPTER
THIRTY-ONE

Eleanor didn't know how to feel as she saw her father with his arm around Anderson's neck, dragging him away from the scrum so the two of them had space to fight. She didn't like to see her father fighting, but at the same time she knew Anderson was a bad man and he had to be stopped. More than anything she wanted her father to be fair, and prayed he wouldn't do anything terrible to Anderson.

Eleanor and Mary watched as both men drew their swords. The noise of the first clash of blades attracted everyone's attention, and hundreds of heads swivelled round to watch. After that first skirmish, the two men backed off and looked at each other again, as if realising they had acted too quickly and now needed to reappraise their opponent. Eleanor's heart was in her mouth; she was frightened for her father's safety. He was bigger than Anderson, but less artful, and no matter what he had experienced before he met Eleanor's mother, she doubted he had Anderson's skill with a sword. She held her breath and waited for the fight to continue, but before Anderson had chance to do anything further, Zoran and Robert appeared from the crowd, bundling Anderson onto the ground.

'Coward!' screamed Anderson. 'Call off your men and fight me yourself.'

'They're your men,' shouted Jonathan in response. 'You trained them.'

The fighting had momentarily stopped. Lucinda had gone to her horse and returned with a long length of rope, which she used to bind Anderson's wrists. From the distance, a rock flew from Katharine's catapult. It caught Lucinda in the side of the face, prompting a sudden, dramatic splattering of blood. She screamed, and Zoran and Robert ran towards Katharine, pushing their way through the crowd. Katharine saw them coming, and turned and tried to run, but the two men were already upon her. Eleanor could see they were furious that Katharine had injured their friend and they were not gentle with her, dragging her from the melee by her hair. She protested and shouted, but they didn't stop until she was alongside Anderson, and her hands were also bound.

Jonathan had suggested that the capture of these two would bring an end to the battle, but this hadn't proved to be the case. Instead, seeing their adult leaders defeated seemed to prompt the children to greater anger, and with a new surge of energy, they resumed fighting. Eleanor and Mary ran down to where most of the Castle Six stood watching, clearly trying to decide what to do next. A soldier from the Baldwin Castle army approached them.

'The twins are in charge,' he said.

'Who?' asked Lucinda. 'Hephzi and Beth?'

The soldier shook his head. 'No. Two boys. The fat, angry ones. If you capture them, the children will be too scared to continue.'

'Where are they?' asked Jonathan.

'At the front of the army. We're doing our best, but they're hard to get to. They've surrounded themselves with the most violent children, and they're psychotic enough on their own.'

'OK,' said Jonathan. 'How can we help?'

'I'll get as many soldiers as possible to attack the phalanx around them. The second they look like they're starting to weaken, you get in and yank them out.'

'They're called Andrew and Stephen,' said Mary, in a quiet voice, 'I can help you distract them.'

Eleanor was surprised, and very pleased, to see her friend offering to help in this way. Mary's words had hurt her, but the whole time she'd been talking, Eleanor had kept reminding herself that her friend was often hot-headed and that she probably didn't mean a lot of what she was saying.

Eleanor stayed with the injured Lucinda as Mary and Jonathan made their way towards the twins. The cut on her cheek didn't look so bad close up, but Eleanor could tell from the way she winced that she was still in considerable pain.

'Shall we sit down?' asked Eleanor.

Lucinda nodded. 'But let's get a little bit further away. By the horses. Where it's safe.'

The two of them walked away from the fighting, occasionally turning back to see what was happening. The twins didn't seem to have noticed Mary and Jonathan, intent only on fighting the soldiers immediately in front of them. Several soldiers in the Baldwin army were injured and backing away, but then a new crowd started to move in from all directions and the activity in the centre of the crowd started to intensify.

Eleanor looked for Hephzibah and Beth, and Michael and Stefan. Hephzibah and Beth were together, but had been separated from Alexandra and Sarah. Now their mission was over, they looked lost, caught up in the fighting without their own weapons. Eleanor beckoned for them to come over. For a moment, Alexandra continued struggling with the child in front of her, then abandoned the tussle and started wading her way towards them. Michael and Stefan, who were further up the bank behind them, noticed this, and abandoned their own battles, trying to get out of the struggling mass.

Eleanor turned back to Lucinda, who, being much taller, had a much better view of the action. 'Is the plan working?'

'I don't know,' Lucinda answered. 'It's hard to see.'

Chapter
Thirty-Two

Mary followed Jonathan further into the crush of bodies. She knew he was relying on her, and hoped she'd be able to distract the twins. Jonathan shoved two children out of the way, and then they were close enough to see the backs of the twins' heads, just in front of the rank of children protecting them.

'Andrew!' she shouted. 'Stephen!'

They didn't respond, too intent on fighting. She took a deep breath and tried again. 'I have a message for you. From Anderson.'

This seemed to work, and Andrew momentarily turned round. In that instant, Jonathan leapt forward, grabbing the twin around his fat neck and yanking him back. Andrew's scared yelps drew Stephen's attention, and he turned round too, giving the Baldwin Castle army the space they needed to get him. Jonathan dragged Andrew through the crowd, the boy's significant weight forcing him to move slowly. Mary followed behind, trying not to get knocked over by the soldiers bringing Stephen. When they finally broke free of the crowd, the two boys tried to run back into the action but were restrained from doing so.

'They're all still fighting,' said Eleanor.

'Wait,' said the soldier and pointed up to the battlements. Moments later a woman appeared holding a large metal cone. When she spoke into it her voice was amplified so most of the crowd could hear it.

'Stop,' she said, 'the battle is over. We have captured Anderson, Katharine, Mary, Andrew and Stephen.'

'I wasn't captured,' said Mary.

'Shhh,' Eleanor urged.

'Those of you who wish to continue to fight can do so, but I promise your efforts will be futile. Our army is stronger than yours. So far we have concentrated only on holding you back. From now on, anyone we capture will be imprisoned in our dungeon along with Andrew and Stephen. And I promise you that our dungeon is not a nice place to be.'

'There,' said the soldier, 'that should do it.'

It took the army of children a long time to disperse. The threat of being imprisoned in the dungeon clearly worked on them, and there was little more conflict, but they hung around for several hours, as if each one of them was frightened of being called a coward, finally setting off in small, separate groups. They reminded Mary of the children who hung about by the river, and she worried about how they would survive in the Kinder Castle without a leader. Mary also felt sorry for Andrew and Stephen, who hadn't stopped crying since their wrists were bound. At first Mary thought the Baldwin Castle had only threatened to imprison the twins and wouldn't go through with it, but now it seemed they would be spending at least a night in the dungeon.

'We can take care of Anderson and Katharine too,' a soldier had told Jonathan.

'No,' he replied, 'they're our responsibility.'

'What about the girl?'

'Mary? She was clearly brainwashed. As soon as she saw her friends she returned to normal and even offered to help. I don't think we can hold her responsible for anything Katharine and Anderson made her do. Even the strongest of us would probably crumble if faced with their techniques.'

Throughout this exchange, Mary remained silent. She might have defended Anderson and Katharine to Eleanor, but she had no desire to have her hands bound and be forced to share a cell with them in the Clearheart Castle's dungeon. It seemed far more sensible to keep quiet and wait to see what would happen.

Later in the afternoon, two women and one men, who weren't part of the army and dressed in fine silk clothing, approached Jonathan.

'You're the Castle Six, aren't you?' one of the women asked.

He nodded.

'We've heard about you. We wondered why you haven't visited our castle and community. You would receive a very warm welcome here.'

Alexandra stepped in. 'Thank you. We are only at the very beginning of our travels, and so far we've concentrated on castles that we already have some connection with. It can be dangerous visiting unknown communities.'

The first woman nodded. 'I understand. But we would appreciate it if you came to see us again. Under happier circumstances.'

'Yes,' said Alexandra, 'we would like that too.'

The trio invited the Castle Six to spend an evening with them, but Jonathan was eager to return to his community. They allowed the Baldwin Castle's doctor to stitch Lucinda's cheek, but as soon as that was done, they mounted their horses and got ready to go. Anderson rode behind Jonathan, his hands still bound; Katharine behind Alexandra. Neither prisoner made any attempt to escape, and the group rode away, hoping to reach an inn before nightfall.

CHAPTER
THIRTY-THREE

The innkeeper was most amused by the challenge of finding somewhere to keep Anderson and Katharine. He suggested the stables might be the best place for them and when Jonathan worried that the rope might not be strong enough to hold them overnight, he returned with some metal chains.

'This should do it,' he laughed. 'I think you'll find them here tomorrow.'

That night, Eleanor asked if she could speak to the Castle Six together.

'Of course,' said Alexandra. 'The children too?'

'No. Just you six.'

'OK. I'll go round everyone up. Come to my room in half an hour.'

Eleanor felt intimidated when she entered Alexandra's room half an hour later as instructed and found all the

Castle Six sitting on the bed waiting for her to speak. But she took three deep breaths, summoned up all her courage and said, 'I think we should let Mary join the group.'

'What?' asked Jonathan. 'She's lucky to have escaped serious punishment. We can't reward her for her bad behaviour.'

'Dad, you said she made up for that when she helped you capture the twins. And I'm not just saying this because she's my friend. She's undergone intensive training with Anderson and Katharine, and she's as skilled as any of the rest of us. Plus, I think it would be better if she was on our side rather than running the risk of her turning on us again.'

'See,' said Jonathan, 'you're admitting you can't trust her. That's not the sort of person we need on our team.'

Eleanor was about to protest when Alexandra said, 'I think Eleanor has a good point. But so does Jonathan. The last thing we want is for the children at our community to believe that if they run away or betray us they'll get to join our group.'

'Mary didn't run away. She was kidnapped. No one knows about what happened between her, Anderson and Katharine. Not back in our community anyway.'

'That's true,' said Alexandra. 'But I think before we can let Mary join our group, we need to have a talk with her. If she's prepared to be mature about this, and swear that she's changed and will never betray us, then I'm prepared to consider Eleanor's suggestion. Eleanor, go find Mary, and send her up to us.'

Eleanor nodded and left Alexandra's bedroom. She went downstairs and found Mary sitting in the games room with Michael and Stefan.

'Where is everyone?' asked Michael. 'Zoran's not playing cards or in the bar, so I know something must be up.'

'They're having a meeting upstairs. Mary, can you go to Alexandra's room?'

'Oh no,' she said, 'am I going to be punished?'

'They just want to talk to you, that's all.'

Mary lifted up her blue hat and swept her red hair back. 'OK,' she said, 'show me where to go.'

Eleanor waited outside Alexandra's bedroom as the Castle Six talked to Mary. It was a long time before she emerged, but when she did she ran straight over and gave Eleanor a kiss on the cheek. Eleanor was pleased, and glad her friend was happy, but she needed Mary to say the right words to make up for everything she had done.

'Eleanor,' Mary began, 'I am so grateful for this. I know they're only allowing me to join because you spoke up for me . . . and I promise you that you won't regret giving me a second chance.'

'Good,' Eleanor replied. 'Because the only way this can work is if we all trust each other.'

'I know,' said Mary, looking down at the floor. 'I can't excuse my behaviour. My head was turned. All that silly stuff I said about being the Queen of England, it was nonsense, I realise that now. Anderson was only saying that to turn me against you. He could see my weak spots, he knew how left out I felt when you disappeared from the community. Please, Eleanor, please forgive me.'

Eleanor was touched by her friend's appeal and gave her a hug. 'I'm sorry I didn't ask them before, Mary. I've always wanted you to be part of this. I just didn't realise it was a possibility. And I'm sorry for having to ask you this, but as I've given my word to the Castle Six, you have to promise me that you will never have any contact with Anderson again . . . and I have to believe you.'

'Oh, Eleanor,' said Mary, 'I can put my hand on my heart and promise you that without any reservation. He's a dangerous man, I know that now, and his compliments mean nothing to me. Only when I earn the Castle Six's praise will I feel that I've achieved something worthwhile.'

Eleanor smiled. 'I'm so pleased to hear you say that, Mary.'

Mary gave her a hard squeeze and said, 'Come on then, let's tell the others.'

CHAPTER THIRTY-FOUR

When Eleanor was awoken by a knock on her bedroom door late that night, she knew it would be Michael. What she didn't know was that he would have such disturbing news.

'Beth has run away.'

'What?'

'She's only just gone. If we go now maybe we can find her.'

'OK, I'll wake the others.'

'No,' said Michael, 'please don't. Not yet. Not until you and I have at least tried to find her.'

Eleanor sighed. 'OK. I'll just put my boots on.'

Everyone in the inn was asleep, and even the bar was empty. Eleanor and Michael tiptoed down the stairs as quietly as possible, afraid of being caught.

'It's all my fault,' Michael admitted. 'But what could I say? I had no idea she had those sorts of feelings about me.'

'Oh,' said Eleanor, 'is that what this is about?'

'You knew how she felt?'

Eleanor nodded.

'And you didn't tell me?'

'I thought you knew. *She* thought you knew. That night at the Kingmaker's Castle, after the Storytellers' performance, when you and she held hands? When we went for a night-time walk I tried to hint to you about her feelings, and the way you responded . . .'

'I knew she was fond of me,' he said, 'but I didn't think she expected me to dump her sister. Oh, Eleanor, I don't know what to do. Or what I should have said. I tried to explain, but she just kept crying and crying . . .'

'Michael, don't worry. It's OK, we'll find her. You've been very brave, not responding to Beth's tactics. And if you gave in to her, things would have been just as bad, only it would've been her sister who was upset.'

He nodded. 'You're right. Only please let's find her.'

They paused at the inn's front door, uncertain whether they would be able to get back in once they'd gone out. Eleanor looked round for something to prop the door open. She found a small block of wood and used it as a doorstop.

'There,' she said, once they were outside, 'now we won't get trapped out here.'

'Where do you think she's gone?'

'There is one possibility, but she wouldn't be that stupid, would she?'

'The stables?'

Eleanor nodded.

She felt afraid as she walked through the stone doorway, worried this might be some sort of trap. Although it seemed unlikely that Beth might have got upset deliberately, if she'd come in here in an angry mood, Katharine and Anderson might have exploited that emotion to persuade her to unchain them.

'There she is,' shouted Michael. 'Over there.'

Eleanor flinched, and then looked where Michael was pointing. Anderson and Katharine were curled up together, and Katharine had her arm around Beth.

'Let her go,' shouted Eleanor.

'Oh, Eleanor,' said Katharine, 'I'm not holding the girl against her will. She just came in here for some comfort. Honestly, you people are so arrogant. You seem able to upset all of your friends without noticing.'

Eleanor was hurt by this, especially after she'd only recently managed to resolve her problems with Mary. But she told herself that Katharine was an expert at exploiting the weaknesses of everyone around her, and, determined not to give in to this, said in a clear voice, as if she was an adult and addressing a child, 'Katharine, this is none of your business.' She looked directly at Beth and said, 'Please, come back with us.'

Beth looked up at them. Her face was red and streaked with tears. 'Why should I?'

'Because you don't want to spend the night in these stables. And things will seem much better in the morning.'

Beth turned to Katharine. 'I do feel stronger now.'

'Then go with them,' she told her. 'Just remember my advice. No boy is worth getting this upset over, especially one who can't see how much prettier you are than your sister.'

Eleanor held out her hand to Beth. She got up from alongside Katharine and walked away from her, deliberately ignoring Eleanor's friendly gesture. Eleanor tried to remain calm. She couldn't tell if Anderson was awake, but if he was, she didn't like the way he remained silent. Together, the three of them returned to the inn.

CHAPTER
THIRTY-FIVE

The inhabitants of the Clearheart Castle community gave the Castle Six a warm welcome on their return. News of Mary's disappearance had spread through almost every home, and everyone was eager to celebrate her safe return. There were more violent groups as well, mobs who wished to tear Anderson and Katharine limb from limb. The community army had to stay alongside them throughout the journey to the castle, blocking the entrance as the couple were taken down to the dungeon.

The community was calmed by a night-long celebration, the climax of which was Mary being bounced high into the sky from a large blue blanket. Her parents were giddy with relief and kept trying to express this to Jonathan and Eleanor. But they found it hard to accept their thanks, worried about the fact that Eleanor's mother April was not at the party. Eleanor suggested they should go home but Jonathan said, 'No. We'll wait until the party's over. Then we'll find out what's wrong with her.'

This worried Eleanor, but she didn't want to argue with her father on this happy occasion and they stayed at the party until dawn. Then they walked back to their house together.

April was waiting for them. She was sitting in a chair covered with a blanket and had clearly been sleeping. Eleanor ran over to her mother, expecting an embrace, but April remained where she was.

'Why didn't you come to the party?' Jonathan asked April.

April didn't answer.

'Mary's safe. We rescued her. Do you care about that?'

'Eleanor,' said April, 'you must be very tired. Can you go to bed, please?'

Eleanor looked at her father. 'It's OK,' he said. 'You get some sleep.'

Eleanor went upstairs to her bedroom. She had suspected her mother was upset, but couldn't believe she had greeted them with such a chilly welcome. But in spite of all her anxiety, Eleanor was exhausted, and soon managed to get to sleep. Whatever was wrong would have to wait.

Chapter Thirty-Six

Eleanor awoke in the late afternoon. Her father stood over her bed and told her, 'A messenger's just arrived for us. We have to go to the castle.'

'OK,' she said.

'The horses are ready. Do you need any breakfast?'

'I wouldn't mind something. An apple, maybe?'

Jonathan smiled and produced the piece of fruit from his pocket.

They went outside and mounted their horses.

'Where's Mum?' asked Eleanor.

'She's sleeping. We had a long talk last night.'

'What's wrong with her?'

He shrugged. 'I don't think she realised how lonely she would be with both of us gone. And she's been really worried about Mary. Frustrated because she hasn't been able to do anything, and we weren't there.'

'But that's not our fault, is it, Dad?'

He shook his head. 'If it's anyone's problem, it's mine. Don't worry, Eleanor, I'm sure it will all be sorted out soon.'

Eleanor nodded, and they rode off.

When they arrived at the castle, they were told to go up to the meeting room on the third level. Everyone else was already waiting for them.

'Jonathan, Eleanor, sit down . . .' said Alexandra. They did so. 'Good. Now, I'm sorry for calling you here when you must still be very tired, but there's just a few loose ends we need to tie up.

'The community sees our last mission as a success. Not because we fostered any bonds with the King-maker's Castle, they don't care about that, but because we rescued Mary and brought home the bad guys. Last night's party was an important celebration, and I think things will be harmonious for a while, but there remains the question of the Kinder Castle. The Baldwin Castle told me that they will release Andrew and Stephen after twenty-four hours, and no doubt they will return home. But as the children have been given military training, and have now tasted battle, I think it would be danger-ous to leave them without an adult leader. So, I've decided to send Robert to rule over them.'

Eleanor turned to look at Robert. He looked proud, smiling back at her.

'Because this is a decision that affects all of us, we need to have a vote. It's a majority vote, and the children's voices are just as important as the adults. So . . . all those in favour?'

For a moment no one did anything. Alexandra prompted them by saying, 'You have to raise your hands.'

Still people seemed uncertain. Robert said, 'It's OK, everybody, I'm happy to go.'

Hearing this, the group became more confident and slowly the adults and children raised their hands until almost everyone had contributed to the positive vote. The only dissenter was Zoran, who kept his hands firmly under his armpits and looked extremely disappointed.

Robert departed immediately after the meeting. He hugged everyone and gave Michael his tunic with the brass bear. Eleanor watched him as he approached Zoran and said, 'It'll be OK – you can come and visit.'

Zoran shrugged. Robert turned to Alexandra. 'Maybe he could go with me? Two leaders would be better than one.'

'No,' she said, 'we can't lose both of you. We've gone from being the Castle Seven to the Castle Five, to drop to the Castle Four would be a sign of terrible weakness to the community. But, Zoran, don't get too upset. This is only a temporary appointment for Robert. You'll see him again, I promise.'

Zoran didn't answer. Robert could tell he wasn't going to get anything out of him and gave up. The goodbyes complete, he mounted his horse and rode away. Eleanor understood why Zoran was sorry to lose his friend and was equally sad to see him go. Robert had been a man of almost as few words as Zoran, except when the pair of them were drunk, but he had brought a good humour to the group and now that he was leaving and Zoran seemed depressed, it was apparent that Lucinda would be the only one who would provide any well-needed lightness of mood.

Jonathan hugged Eleanor and said, 'Time to go.'

She nodded.

'Be nice to your mum, OK? It's hard for her.'

'I will, Dad. I promise.'

He smiled. 'You're a good daughter, Eleanor. I'm proud of you.'

Eleanor didn't know what to say, so she gave her father a big hug back and they walked over to their horses, both exhausted from the excitement of the last few days and looking forward to a much-needed rest.

 ACKNOWLEDGEMENTS

Special thanks to fellow castle-dwellers, Alexandra
Heminsley and Lesley Thorne